THE ORIGINAL ADVENTURES OF

Hank

THE
COWDOG.

John R. Erickson

Illustrations by Gerald L. Holmes

Maverick Books
Published by Gulf Publishing Company
Houston, Texas

Maverick Books
Published by Gulf Publishing Company
P.O. Box 2608 Houston, Texas 77252-2608

10   9   8   7   6

Library of Congress Cataloging-in-Publication Data

Erickson, John R., 1943–
  The original adventures of Hank the Cowdog/
John R. Erickson.
        p.   cm.
  Summary: Hank the Cowdog, Head of Ranch
Security, is framed for the murder of a chicken and
becomes an outlaw with the coyotes.
  ISBN 0-87719-131-X (hbk.).—ISBN 0-87719-130-1
(pbk.).—ISBN 0-87719-149-2 (cassette)
  1. Dogs—Fiction. [1. Dogs—Fiction. 2. West
(U.S.)—Fiction. 3. Humorous stories.]   I. Title.   II.
Title: Hank the Cowdog. PS3555.R428075   1991
813'.54—dc20   91-6731
                                                    CIP
                                                    AC

Book and cover design by Tom Hair.

Printed in the United States of America.

Hank the Cowdog is a registered trademark
of John R. Erickson.

Contents

Have you read all of Hank's adventures?
Available in paperback at $6.95:

All books are available on audio cassette too!
($15.95 for two cassettes)

Also available on cassettes:
Hank the Cowdog's Greatest Hits!

CHAPTER

1

BLOODY MURDER

It's me again, Hank the Cowdog. I just got some terrible news. There's been a murder on the ranch.

I know I shouldn't blame myself. I mean, a dog is only a dog. He can't be everywhere at once. When I took this job as Head of Ranch Security, I knew that I was only flesh and blood, four legs, a tail, a couple of ears, a pretty nice kind of nose that the women really go for, two bushels of hair and another half-bushel of Mexican sandburs.

You add that all up and you don't get Superman, just me, good old easy-going Hank who works hard, tries to do his job, and gets very little cooperation from anyone else around here.

I'm not complaining. I knew this wouldn't

be an easy job. It took a special kind of dog—strong, fearless, dedicated, and above all, smart. Obviously Drover didn't fit. The job fell on my shoulders. It was my destiny. I couldn't escape the broom of history that swept through . . . anyway, I took the job.

Head of Ranch Security. Gee, I was proud of that title. Just the sound of it made my tail wag. But now this, a murder, right under my nose. I know I shouldn't blame myself, but I do.

I got the report this morning around dawn. I had been up most of the night patrolling the northern perimeter of ranch headquarters. I had heard some coyotes yapping up there and I went up to check it out. I told Drover where I was going and he came up lame all of a sudden, said he needed to rest his right front leg.

I went alone, didn't find anything. The coyotes stayed out in the pasture. I figured there were two, maybe three of them. They yapped for a couple of hours, making fun of me, calling me ugly names, and daring me to come out and fight.

Well, you know me. I'm no dummy. There's a thin line between heroism and stupidity, and I try to stay on the south side of it. I didn't go out and fight, but I answered them bark for bark, yap for yap, name for name.

The coyote hasn't been built who can out-yap Hank the Cowdog.

A little before dawn, Loper, one of the cow-boys on this outfit, stuck his head out the door and bellered, "Shut up that yapping, you idiot!" I guess he thought there was only one coyote out there.

They kept it up and I gave it back to them. Next time Loper came to the door, he was armed. He fired a gun into the air and squalled, something about how a man couldn't sleep around here with all the dad-danged noise. I agreed.

Would you believe it? Them coyotes yipped louder than ever, and I had no choice but to give it back to them.

Loper came back out on the porch and fired another shot. This one came so close to me that I heard the hum. Loper must have lost his bearings or something, so I barked louder than ever to give him my position, and, you know, to let him know that I was out there protecting the ranch.

The next bullet just derned near got me. I mean, I felt the wind of it as it went past. That was enough for me. I shut her down for the night. If Loper couldn't aim any better than that, he was liable to hurt somebody.

I laid low for a while, hiding in the shelter belt, until I was sure the artillery had gone back to bed. Then I went down for a roll in the sewer, cleaned up, washed myself real good, came out feeling refreshed and ready to catch up on my sleep. Trotted down to the gas tanks and found Drover curled up in my favorite spot.

I growled him off my gunny sack. "Beat it, son. Make way for the night patrol."

He didn't want to move so I went to sterner measures, put some fangs on him. That moved him out, and he didn't show no signs of lameness either. I have an idea that where Drover is lamest is between his ears.

I did my usual bedtime ritual of walking in a tight circle around my bed until I found just exactly the spot I wanted, and then I flopped down. Oh, that felt good! I wiggled around and finally came to rest with all four paws sticking up in the air. I closed my eyes and had some wonderful twitching dreams about . . . don't recall exactly the subject matter, but most likely they were about Beulah, the neighbor's collie. I dream about her a lot.

What a woman! Makes my old heart pound just to think about her. Beautiful brown and white hair, big eyes, nose that tapers down to a point (not quite as good as mine, but so what?), and nice ears that flap when she runs.

Only trouble is that she's crazy about a spotted bird dog, without a doubt the ugliest, dumbest, worthlessest cur I ever met. What could be uglier than a spotted short-haired dog with a long skinny tail? And what could be dumber or more worthless than a dog that goes around chasing *birds*?

They call him Plato. I don't know why, except maybe because his eyes look like plates half the time, empty plates. He don't know a cow from a sow, but do you think that makes him humble? No sir. He thinks that bird-chasing is hot stuff. What really hurts, though, is that Beulah seems to agree.

Don't understand that woman, but I dream about her a lot.

Anyway, where was I? Under the gas tanks, catching up on my sleep. All at once Drover was right there beside me, jumping up and down and giving off that high-pitched squeal of his that kind of bores into your eardrums. You can't ignore him when he does that.

Well, I throwed open one eye, kept the other one shut so that I could get some halfway sleep. ''Will you please shut up?''

"Hank, oh Hankie, it's just terrible, you wouldn't believe, hurry and wake up, I seen his tracks down on the creek, get up before he escapes!"

I throwed open the other eye, pushed myself up, and went nose-to-nose with the noise-maker. "Quit hopping around. Quit making all that racket. Hold still and state your business."

"Okay Hank, all right, I'll try." He tried and was none too successful, but he did get the message across. "Oh Hank, there's been a killing, right here on the ranch, and we slept through it!"

"Huh?" I was coming awake by then, and the word *killing* sent a jolt clean out to the end of my tail. "Who's been killed?"

"They hit the chickenhouse, Hank. I don't know how they got in but they did, busted in there and killed one of those big leghorn hens, killed her dead, Hank, and oh, the blood!"

Well, that settled it. I had no choice but to go back on duty. A lot of dogs would have just turned over and gone back to sleep, but I take this stuff pretty serious.

We trotted up to the chickenhouse, and Drover kept jumping up and down and talking. "I found some tracks down by the creek.

I'm sure they belong to the killer, Hank, I'm just sure they do."

"What kind of tracks?"

"Coyote."

"Hmm." We reached the chickenhouse and, sure enough, there was the hen lying on the ground, and she was still dead. I walked around the body, sniffing it good and checking the signs.

I noticed the position of the body and memorized every detail. The hen was lying on her left side, pointing toward the northeast, with one foot out and the other one curled up under her wing. Her mouth was open and it appeared to me that she had lost some tail feathers.

"Uh huh, I'm beginning to see the pattern."

"What, tell me, Hank, who done it?"

"Not yet. Where'd you see them tracks?" There weren't any tracks around the corpse, ground was too hard. Drover took off in a run and I followed him down into the brush along the creek.

He stopped and pointed to some fresh tracks in the mud. "There they are, Hank, just where I found them. Are you proud of me?"

I pushed him aside and studied the sign,

looked it over real careful, sniffed it, gave it the full treatment. Then I raised up.

"Okay, I've got it now. It's all clear. Them's coon tracks, son, not coyote. I can tell from the scent. Coons must have attacked while I was out on patrol. They're sneaky, you've got to watch 'em every minute."

Drover squinted at the tracks. "Are you sure those are coon tracks? They sure look like coyote to me."

"You don't go by the *look,* son, you go by the *smell.* This nose of mine don't lie. If it says coon, you better believe there's a coon at the end of them tracks. And I'm fixing to clean house on him. Stay behind me and don't get hurt."

I threaded my way through the creek willows, over the sand, through the water. I never lost the scent. In the heat of a chase, all my senses come alive and point like a blazing arrow toward the enemy.

In a way I felt sorry for the coon, even though he'd committed a crime and become my mortal enemy. With me on his trail, the little guy just didn't have a chance. One of the disadvantages of being as big and deadly as I am is that you sometimes find yourself in sympathy with the other guy.

But part of being Head of Ranch Security is learning to ignore that kind of emotion. I mean, to hold down this job, you have to be cold and hard.

The scent was getting stronger all the time, and it didn't smell exactly like any coon I'd come across before. All at once I saw him. I stopped dead still and Drover, the little dummy, ran right into me and almost had a heart attack. I guess he thought I was a giant coon or something. It's hard to say what he thinks.

The coon was hiding in some bushes about five feet in front of me. I could hear him chewing on something, and that smell was real strong now.

''What's that?'' Drover whispered, sniffing the air.

''Coon, what do you think?'' I glanced back at him. He was shaking with fear. ''You ready for some combat experience?''

''Yes,'' he squeaked.

''All right, here's the plan. I'll jump him and try to get him behind the neck. You come in the second wave and take what you can. If you run away like you did last time, I'll sweep the corral with you and give you a whupping you won't forget. All right, let's move out.''

I crouched down and crept forward, every

muscle in my highly conditioned body taut and ready for action. Five feet, four feet, three feet, two. I sprang through the air and hit right in the middle of the biggest porcupine I ever saw.

C H A P T E R

2

QUILLS: JUST PART OF THE JOB

It was kind of a short fight. Coming down, I seen them quills aimed up at me and tried to change course. Too late. I don't move so good in mid-air.

I lit right in the middle of him and *bam,* he slapped me across the nose with his tail, sure did hurt too, brought tears to my eyes. I hollered for Drover to launch the second wave but he had disappeared.

Porcupine took another shot at me but I dodged, tore up half an acre of brush, and got the heck out of there. As I limped back up to the house on pin-cushion feet, my thoughts went back to the murder scene and the evidence I had committed to memory.

It was clear now. The porcupine had had

11

nothing at all to do with the murder because porcupines don't eat anything but trees. Drover had found the first set of tracks he had come to and had started hollering about coyotes. I had been duped into believing the runt.

Yes, it was all clear. I had no leads, no clues, no idea who had killed the hen. What I *did* have was a face-full of porcupine quills, as well as several in my paws.

I limped up to the yard gate. As you might expect, Drover was nowhere to be seen. I sat down beside the gate and waited for Loper to come out and remove the quills.

A lot of dogs would have set up a howl and a moan. Not me. I figgered that when a dog got to be Head of Ranch Security, he ought to be able to stand some pain. It just went with the territory.

So I waited and waited and Loper didn't come out. Them quills was beginning to hurt. The end of my nose throbbed, felt like a balloon. Made me awful restless, but I didn't whine or howl.

Pete the barn cat came along just then, had his tail stuck straight up in the air and was rubbing along the fence, coming my way. He had his usual dumb-cat expression and I could hear him purring.

He came closer. I glared at him. "Scram, cat."

He stopped, arched his back, and rubbed up against the fence. "What's that on your face?"

"Nothing you need to know about."

He rubbed and purred, then reached up and sharpened his claws on a post. "You sure look funny with all those things sticking out of your nose."

"You're gonna look funny if you don't run along and mind your own business. I'm not in the mood to take any of your trash right now."

He grinned and kept coming, started rubbing up against my leg. I decided to ignore him, look the other way and pretend he wasn't there. Sometimes that's the best way to handle a cat, let him know that you won't allow him to get you stirred up. You have to be firm with cats. Give 'em the slightest encouragement and they'll try to move in and take over.

Pete rubbed and purred. I ignored him, told myself he wasn't there. Then he brought that tail up and flicked it across the end of my nose. I curled my lip and growled. He looked up at me and did it again.

It tickled my nose, made my eyes water. I had to sneeze. I tried to fight it back but couldn't hold it. I gave a big sneeze and them quills sent fire shooting through my nose, kind of inflamed me, don't you see, and all at once I lost my temper.

I made a snap at him but he was gone, over the fence and into Sally May's yard, which is sort of off limits to us dogs even though Pete can come and go as he pleases, which ain't fair.

With the fence between us, Pete knew he was safe. He throwed a hump into his back and hissed, and what was I supposed to do then? Sing him a lullaby? Talk about the weather? No sir, I barked. I barked hard and loud, just to let that cat know that he couldn't get *me* stirred up.

The door opened and Loper stepped out on the porch. He was wearing jeans and an undershirt, no hat and no boots, and he had a cup of coffee in his hand.

"Hank! Leave the cat alone!"

I stopped and stared at him. *Leave the cat alone!* Pete grinned and walked off, purring and switching the tip of his tail back and forth.

I could have killed him.

I whined and wagged my tail and went over to the gate where Loper could see my nose. He looked up at the sky, took a drink of coffee, swatted a mosquito on his arm, looked up at the clouds again. I whined louder and jumped on the gate so that he couldn't miss seeing that old Hank, his loyal friend and protector of the ranch, had been wounded in the line of duty.

"Don't jump on the gate." He yawned and went back into the house.

Twenty minutes later he came out again, dressed for the day's work. I had waited patiently. My nose was really pounding by this time, but I didn't complain. When he came out the gate, I jumped up to greet him.

Know what he said? "Hank, you stink! Have you been in the sewer again?" And he walked on down to the corral, didn't see the quills in my nose.

At last he saw them. We were down at the corral. He shook his head and muttered, "Hank, when are you going to learn about porcupines? How many times do we have to go through this? Drover never gets quills in his nose."

Well, Drover was a little chicken and Loper just didn't understand. Nobody understood.

© 1982
G.L. Holmes

He got a pair of fencing pliers out of the saddle shed, threw a leg lock on me, and started
pulling. It hurt. Oh it hurt! Felt like he was
pulling off my whole nose. But I took it without a whimper—well, maybe I whimpered a
little bit—and we got 'er done.

Loper rubbed me behind the ears. "There,
now try to stay away from porcupines." He
stood up and started to dust off his jeans when
he noticed the wet spot.

His eyes came up and they looked kind of
wrathful. "Did you do that?"

I was well on my way to tall timber when he

threw the pliers at me.

I couldn't help it. I didn't do it on purpose. The quills just got to hurting so bad that I had to let something go. Was it my fault that he had me in a leg lock and got in the way?

Make one little mistake around this ranch and they nail you to the wall.

I laid low for a while, hid in the post pile and nursed my nose. It was about ten o'clock when Sally May discovered the murdered hen.

CHAPTER
3

AN ENORMOUS MONSTER

I debated for a long time about what to do next. Should I hide out and play it safe, or go on down to the chickenhouse and get blamed for something that wasn't my fault?

Curiosity got the best of me and I trotted down to see what was going on.

Drover was already there when I arrived, wagging his stub tail and trying to win a few points with his loyal dog routine. I walked up to him and said, out of the corner of my mouth, "Thanks for all the help this morning. I really appreciate it."

I think he missed the note of irony, because he said—and I mean with a straight face—he said, "That's okay, Hankie, it wasn't nothing."

Dang right it wasn't nothing.

Loper was kneeling over the hen, studying the signs. Sally May stood nearby, looking mighty unhappy about the dead chicken. Loper pushed his hat to the back of his head and stood up. His eyes went straight to me and Drover, only when I glanced around, I noticed that Drover had disappeared. It was just me, standing in the spotlight.

"Hank, if you hadn't been out barking all night, you might have prevented this. Why do you think we keep you around here?" I hung my head and tucked my tail. "Do you have any idea how much money it costs to keep you dogs around here? Seems that every time I turn around I'm having to buy another fifty pound sack of dog food. That stuff's expensive."

Maybe this ain't the time or place to argue the point, but just for the record let me say that Co-op dog food is the cheapest you can buy. I don't know what they make it out of—hulls, straw, sawdust, anything the pigs won't eat, and then they throw in a little grease to give it a so-called flavor. Tastes like soap and about half the time it gives me an upset stomach.

The point is, I wasn't exactly eating the ranch into bankruptcy. Thought I ought to throw that in to give a more balanced view of things.

Loper went on. "We can't afford to keep you dogs around here if you're going to let this sort of thing go on. Everybody has to earn his keep on the ranch. I don't want this to happen again."

What did he suppose *I* wanted? Sometimes I just don't understand . . . oh well.

He picked up the dead chicken by the feet and carried it down to the trash barrel. I got to admit that I watched this with some interest, since it had occurred to me that there wasn't much any of us could do for the dead chicken.

The more I thought about chicken dinner, the more my mouth watered. Couldn't get it off my mind. I like chicken about as well as any food you can name. Has a nice clean taste except for the feathers. Feathers are pretty tasteless, if you ask me, and they kind of scrape when they go down.

Sure was hungry for chicken, but I decided against it. Wouldn't look too good if I got caught eating the murder victim, after all the trouble I'd gotten into that day.

I tried to concentrate on the scene of the crime. I studied it again, went over the ground and sniffed it out. Nothing, no clues, no tracks, no scent. Could have been a coyote, a coon, a skunk, a badger, even a fox.

But there was one thing I was sure of. It wouldn't happen again, not while I was in charge of security, not as long as I could still stand up and fight for the ranch.

I saw Drover peek his head out of the machine shed. "Get some sleep, son," I told him. 'Tonight we throw up a double guard, and we could get ourselves into some combat."

We slept till dark. When the moon came up, we went out on patrol, made several laps around headquarters. Everything was quiet. Off in the distance we heard a few coyotes, but they weren't anywhere close.

Must have been after midnight when Drover said his feet hurt, he wanted to rest a while. I left him in front of the chickenhouse and told him to sound the alarm if he saw anything unusual. I went on down and checked things at the corral, made the circle around the place, and ended up back at the chickenhouse about half an hour later.

Thought I'd drop in unannounced and check on Drover, make sure he was taking care of business. As I sneaked up, I could see him in the moonlight. His ears were perked. He'd take about two steps and pounce on something with his front paws. Then he'd take two more steps and pounce again.

He wasn't paying a lick of attention to the chickenhouse. A guy could have driven a truck in there, loaded up all the hens, and been gone before Drover ever got the news.

I walked up behind him. "What are you doing?"

He screeched and headed for the machine shed. I called him back. He came out, looking all around with big eyes. "Is that you, Hank?"

"Uh huh. What were you doing?"

"Me? Oh nuthin."

It was then that I saw the toad frog jump. "Playing with a toad frog? On guard duty? When we got a murderer running around loose?"

He hung his head and went to wagging that stub tail of his. "I got bored, Hank."

"Sit down, son, me and you need to have a serious talk." He sat down and I marched back and forth in front of him. "Drover, I'm really disappointed in you. When you came to this ranch, you said you wanted to be a cowdog. I had misgivings at the time. I mean, you didn't look like a cowdog. But I took you on anyway and tried to teach you the business. Can you imagine how it breaks my heart to come up here and find you playing with a dad-gummed toad frog?''

His head sank lower and lower, and he started to sniffle.

"If you had gone into any other line of work, playing with a frog would be all right, but a cowdog is something special. You might say we're the elite. We have to be stronger, braver, and tougher than any brand of dog in the world. It's a special calling, Drover, it ain't for the common run of mutts.''

He started crying.

"Drover, there's only one thing that keeps you from being a good cowdog.''

"What is it, Hank?''

"You're worthless.''

"Oh no,'' he squalled, "don't say it! It hurts too much.''

"But it's true. I've tried to be patient, I've tried to teach you, I've tried to be a good example.''

"I know.''

"But it hasn't worked. You're just as worthless today as you were the first time I saw you.''

"Oh-h-h!''

"You're just a chicken-hearted little mutt, is

what you are, and I don't think you'll ever make a cowdog."

"Yes I will, Hank, I just need some time."

"Nope. Duty's duty. I got no choice but to let you go."

He broke down and sobbed. "Oh Hank, I got no place to go, no friends, no family. Nobody wants a chicken-hearted mutt. Give me just three more chances."

"Can't do it, Drover, sorry."

"Two more?"

"Nope."

"One more?"

I paced back and forth. It was one of the most difficult decisions of my career and I didn't want to rush into it.

"All right, one more chance. But one more dumb stunt and you're finished, and I mean forever. Now dry your eyes, shape up, pay attention to your business, and concentrate on being unworthless."

"Okay, Hank." He started jumping up and down and going around in circles. "You won't be sorry. No more frogs for me. I'll guard that chickenhouse and give my life if necessary."

"That's the spirit. I'm going to make the rounds again. If you see anything suspicious, give a holler."

I started off on my rounds and left him sitting in front of the chickenhouse door. I was down at the feed room, checking for coons, when I heard him sound the alarm.

I turned on my incredible speed and went tearing up the hill. I have several speeds, don't you see: slow, normal, and incredible. I save the last one back for special emergencies. When I turn on the incredible speed, I appear as a streak of color moving across the ground. Anything that gets in my way is knocked aside, often destroyed, and I'm not talking about little stuff either. I mean trees, posts, big rocks, you name it.

As I was streaking up the hill, I met Drover. "Hank, I seen him, he's up there, my gosh!"

I had to slow down. "Give me a description."

"Big, Hank, and I mean *BIG,* huge, enormous. Black and white, gigantic tail that whistles through the air, long pointed tongue that flicks out at you, and horns growing out of his head."

"Good grief," I whispered, "what is it?"

"It's a *monster,* Hank, a gen-u-wine monster!"

I stopped to think it over. I'd never tangled

with a monster before. "You think I can whip him?"

"I don't know, Hank. But if anybody can, it's you."

"You're right. Okay, here's the plan. I'll go in the first wave, make the first contact. We'll hold you in reserve. If I holler for help, you come running, get in there with them teeth of yours and bite something. Got that?"

"I got it."

I took a deep breath. "And Drover, if I don't come back from this one, you'll have to go on alone. Take care of the ranch and be brave."

It was kind of a touching moment, me and Drover standing there in the moonlight just before the big battle. I said goodbye and loped up the hill.

I stopped and peered into the gloom. At first I couldn't see anything, but then my eyes fell on a huge shadowy thing standing right in front of the chickenhouse door.

Drover hadn't exaggerated. It was a horned monster, all right, and he was fixing to bust down the door and start killing chickens. I didn't have a moment to waste. It was now or never, him or me, glory or death. I bared my fangs and attacked.

First contact was made only a matter of seconds after I launched the attack. The monster
must have heard me coming, cause he kicked
the tar out of me and sent me rolling. I leaped
up and charged again but this time I made it
through, sank my teeth into him and gave him

a ferocious bite. He slung me around, but I hung on.

He was big, all right, big as a house. I figgered he stood, oh, fourteen feet tall at the shoulder, had three eyes, a long forked tongue, and a tail with deadly stingers on the end of it, also horns that glowed in the dark. And tusks. Did I mention that? Big long tusks growing out of the side of his mouth, the kind that could rip a dog to shreds. Green slobber dripped out of his mouth and his eyes were red.

It was a fight to the death. "Come on, Drover, attack!" I set up a howl to alert the house. I would need all the help I could get.

I'll give Drover credit. He came tearing out of the weeds, yapping at the top of his lungs, and got within three feet of the monster before he veered off and headed for the machine shed.

The lights came on down at the house. The door slammed and I heard Loper running toward me. I hoped he had the gun. I was getting beat up and tired. I wasn't sure I could keep up the fight much longer.

The gun exploded, lit up the night. The monster ran and I started after him, ready to give him the *coop de grass,* as we say, but

Loper called me back. I figgered he didn't want to risk losing the Head of Ranch Security, which seemed pretty sensible to me.

So I went back to him, limping on all four legs at once because they all hurt, and so did everything else. Wagging my tail, I went up to him, ready for my reward.

I didn't get no reward. To make a long story short, Drover had sent me into battle against the milk cow and I got cursed for it.

I thought very seriously about terminating Drover—I mean his life, not his job—but I couldn't find him in the machine shed. So I dragged my battered carcass down to the gas tanks and curled up on my gunny sack bed.

I could have sworn that was a monster.

C H A P T E R

4

THE BOXER

I slept late the next morning. To be real honest about it, I didn't wake up till sometime in the early afternoon. Guess all that monster fighting kind of wore me down.

What woke me up was the sound of the flatbed pickup rattling up to the gas tank, right in front of my bedroom. Loper got out and started filling the pickup. He looked at me, gave his head a shake, and said something under his breath. I tried to read his lips but couldn't make out what he said. Probably wasn't the Pledge of Allegiance.

Slim went around to the front of the pickup and opened up the hood. I was just getting up, right in the middle of a nice stretch, when I heard him say, "Hank, come here, boy."

Geeze, at last a friendly voice. How long had

it been since someone had spoken to me in a kind voice? In my job, nobody ever says a word when you do something right, only when you make a mistake, and then you hear plenty about it.

I trotted around to the front of the pickup —limped, actually, because I was pretty stove up from the battle—wagged my tail and said howdy. Slim bent down and rubbed me behind the ears.

"Good dog," he said.

Good dog! I just melted on those words, rolled over on my back, and kicked all four legs in the air. It's amazing what a few kind words and a smile can do for a dog. Even as hardboiled as I am, which is something you have to be in my line of work, I respond to kindness.

Slim rubbed me in that special place at the bottom of my ribs, the one that's somehow hooked up to my back leg. I've never understood the mechanics of it, but if a guy scratches me there it makes my back leg start kicking.

Slim scratched and I kicked. Felt good and made Old Slim laugh. Then he told me to sit. I sat and tried to shake hands. Shaking hands is one of the many tricks I've learned over the years, and I can usually count on it to delight an audience of people.

But Slim didn't notice. He reached under the hood, pulled out the dipstick, and wiped it off on my ear. "Good dog." And that was it. I waited around for some more scratching or hand-shaking, but he seemed to forget that I was there. He slammed the hood and stepped on my paw. "Oops, sorry Hank, get out of the way."

The sweet moments in this life are fleeting. You have to enjoy them to the fullest when they come, before some noodle steps on you and tells you to get out of the way.

Slim and Loper got into the pickup, and Loper said, "Don't you dogs try to follow us."

He gunned the motor and pulled away from the gas tank. Drover suddenly appeared out of nowhere and hopped up into the back of the pickup.

"Come on, Hank, we're supposed to go."

In the back of my mind I knew that wasn't right, but I didn't have time to think about it. I chased the pickup until it slowed down for the big hill in front of the house, and jumped up in the back.

"Where we going?" I asked.

Drover gave me that famous empty-headed look of his, the one where you can gaze into his eyes and see all the way to the end of his tail, and there's nothing in between. "Beats me, but I bet we're going somewhere."

Loper drove up to the mailbox and turned left. If he had turned right, it would have meant that we were going to the pasture. A left turn meant only one thing: we were going to town. And that meant only one thing: Loper was going to be mad as thunder when he found out we'd jumped in the back and hitched a ride.

But what the heck? You can't be safe and cautious all the time. If you're too timid in this life, you'll miss out on all the fun and adventure. You'll just stay home and snap at the flies, and when you get to be an old dog, you'll look back on your life and think, "All these years I've been on this earth, and I've never done anything but snap at flies."

And you'll regret that, when the opportunity came up, you didn't sneak a ride into town.

Drover curled up behind the cab and watched the scenery go by. I sat on my haunches, closed my eyes, and just let the wind flap my ears around. Felt good, restful. There for a little while I forgot all my cares and responsibilities.

That lasted until we got to the highway. Loper pulled onto the blacktop and started picking up speed. The wind began to sting and my ears flapped a little harder than I like them to flap, and the crumbs of alfalfa hay on the pickup bed started to swirl.

I laid down beside Drover. "Say, before I forget, I want to thank you for all the help you gave me last night with that monster."

He gave me a shy grin. "Oh, that's okay. It was the least I could do."

"It sure as heck was. If you'd done any leaster, you'd have been fighting for the other side."

The shy grin disappeared. "You mad about something?"

"Forget it." I didn't want to talk. Alfalfa leaves were getting into my mouth. I slept all the way to town.

Next thing I knew, we had slowed down and were coasting down Main Street. I sat up and took in the sights: a bunch of stores and street lights, several stop signs, couple of town dogs loafing around, and a big tumbleweed rolling down the middle of the street.

Loper drove into a parking place in front of the Waterhole Cafe, beside two or three other pickups that looked like cowboy rigs. When he got out and saw us back there, he gave us the tongue-lashing I had expected. It was no worse than usual, not bad enough to make me regret that we'd hitched a ride to town.

He told us to sit, be good, and don't bark. Then he and Slim went into the Waterhole.

For five or ten minutes we concentrated on being good, which was a real drag. Then I heard Drover go, "Ps-s-s-st!" He jerked his head toward the pickup that was parked next to us. In the back end, fast asleep, was a big ugly boxer dog. We both moved to the side of the pickup bed and stared at him.

He must have felt our eyes because after a bit his head came up, and he glowered at us with a wicked expression on his face.

"What are you staring at?"

"Just looking at the sights," I said. "What's your name?"

"Puddin' Tane, ask me again and I'll tell you the same."

I guess Drover didn't understand what that meant, so he asked, "What's your name?"

"John Brown, ask me again and I'll knock you down."

Drover gave me a puzzled look, and I said, "How come they've got you chained up?" He was tied to the headache racks of the pickup with a piece of chain.

"So I won't kill any dogs."

"You kill dogs, no fooling?" Drover asked.

"Just for drill. I prefer bigger stuff."

That sort of ended the conversation. Puddin' Tane went back to sleep and I got involved with a couple of noisy flies that were bothering my ears. Took a few snaps at 'em but didn't get anything.

Next thing I knew, Drover said, "What would you do if we peed on your tires?"

The boxer's head came up real slow, and he turned them wicked eyes on little Drover. "What did you say?"

"I said, what would you do if we peed on your tires?"

"Uh Drover . . ." It made me a little uneasy, the way he was talking about *we*.

The boxer sat up. "I'd tear off your legs and wring your neck."

"But how could you do that when you're chained up?"

"Drover."

The boxer lifted one side of his mouth and unveiled a set of long white teeth. "I'd bust the chain."

"It looks pretty stout to me."

"*Drover.*"

"It ain't stout enough."

"Just curious," said Drover. Big-and-Ugly went back to sleep and I got back to them flies. One of them was big and green, also a little slow on the draw. I waited for my shot and snapped. Got the little booger! Then I had to spit him out real quick. Boy, did he taste foul.

Seemed to me I heard water running somewhere. I glanced around and saw Big-and-Ugly's head come up. He'd heard it too.

Drover had just wiped out the left rear tire and was going toward the front one. Seemed to me this was poor judgment on Drover's part.

The boxer sprang to his feet. "Get away from that tire, runt! No two-bit cowdog is going to mess up my tires!"

I didn't like his tone of voice. I got up and wandered to the side of the pickup. "Say there, partner, maybe I didn't hear you right. You weren't suggesting that there's any two-bit cowdogs around here, were you?"

WATER HOLE 83

Special! TUF Chewing Tobacco

© G.L. Holmes
1982

"I ain't suggesting, Buddy, I'm *saying*. You're a couple of two-bit cowdogs."

"Do you mean that as an insult or a compliment?"

"Cowdog don't mean but one thing to me: sorry and two-bit."

I took a deep breath. "Oh dear. Drover, the

dust seems kind of bad all of a sudden. Why don't you wet down that other tire."

He grinned, hiked up his leg, and let 'er rip.

The boxer went nuts when he saw that. All at once his fangs were flashing in the sunlight. He lunged against the chain and started barking—big, deep roar of a bark, so loud you could feel it bouncing off your face.

I waited for him to shut up. "You want to take back what you said about cowdogs?" He lunged against the chain and slashed the air about six inches from the end of my nose. "I guess not."

I hopped down, skipped around to the right side of the boxer's pickup, and wiped out the front and back tires. Drover and I met at the front, swapped sides, and gave each tire a second coat.

Big-and-Ugly went berserk. He fought against the chain and roared. "Let me at 'em, I'll kill 'em, just let me at 'em!"

Drover and I finished the job and hopped back into the pickup bed. When the cafe door burst open, we were, ahem, fast asleep. Slim, Loper, and the boxer's master stormed out.

"What's going on out here? You dogs . . ."

"It's my dog, Loper, he's making all the

racket. Bruno, shut up! You're disturbing the whole town."

I sat up and opened my eyes. Bruno was getting a good scolding from his master. He whined and wagged his stump tail and tried to explain what had happened. But his master didn't understand. (This seems to be a common trait in masters.)

"Now you lie down and be quiet. I don't want to hear another peep out of you. You know better than that."

The men went back inside. I waited a minute and then gave Drover the coast-is-clear sign. We got up and went over to the edge of the pickup. Bruno was lying flat, with his eyes wide open and a couple of fangs showing beneath his lips. He was trembling with rage.

"Drover, you ever seen an uglier dog than that one?"

He giggled. "No, never did."

"Me neither. Can you imagine what his mother must have looked like?"

A growl came from deep in Bruno's throat.

"I don't like his pointed ears," said Drover.

"You know why they're pointed, don't you? When boxers are born, they have such big floppy ears that a surgeon has to cut off two yards of hide. And then they whack off the tail, and then they put the pup's face into a shop vice and mash it until it looks just like Bruno's."

"No kidding?"

"Yup. And as you might expect, it affects the brain too, mashes it down to the size of a dog biscuit." The growl in Bruno's throat was growing louder. "That's why boxers are so dumb, brain's been smallered. It's the mark of the breed. They tell me that you can't get papers on a boxer unless he's too dumb to walk across the street. They give 'em a test, see, and all the ones that flunk become registered boxers."

By this time the growl had become a steady roar.

"And that's why you never see boxers working cattle, just too frazzling dumb to hold down a steady job."

Bruno's eyes were cloudy, as if they were filled with smoke from a fire burning inside. His teeth were snapping together. Maybe he was crushing imaginary bones.

"Why would anybody want a dog that was so big and dumb and ugly?" Drover asked.

"I've wondered about that myself," said I, "and the only answer I can come up with is that maybe if a guy had a piece of log chain that he didn't know what to do with, he'd buy a boxer to hang it on."

That did it. Bruno erupted again and lunged at us, his mouth wide open and full of jagged teeth. I got a real good look at his tonsils, which appeared to be a little inflamed.

I jerked my head at Drover and we was both sending up a line of Z's when the cowboys came out again.

"Bruno, what in the world! Bad dog, bad dog! Why can't you just lie still and shut up like these other dogs?" Bruno whimpered. "Well, I guess I'd better go. Bruno's on a snort. See y'all later."

When the pickup drove off, me and Drover sat up and grinned and waved goodbye to our new friend. Bruno was so mad his eyes were crossed and foam dripped off his chops.

That's what makes being a cowdog worth-while. Teamwork.

C H A P T E R

5

ANOTHER BLOODY
MURDER

When we crossed the cattleguard that put us back on the ranch, I felt a change come over me.

In town I had been just another happy-go-lucky dog without a care in the world. But back on the ranch, I felt that same crushing sense of responsibility that's known to people in high places, such as presidents, prime ministers, emperors, and such. Being Head of Ranch Security is a great honor but also a dreadful burden.

I remembered the chickenhouse murder. I still didn't have any suspects, or I had too many suspects, maybe that was it. Everyone was a suspect, well, everyone but the milk cow, and I had pretty muchly scratched her off the list. And the porcupine, since they only eat trees.

But every other creature on the ranch was under the shadow of suspicion. Except Drover. He was too chicken to kill a chicken.

When we got home, I trotted up to the chickenhouse and went over the whole thing in my mind. While I was sitting there, lost in thought, a chicken came up and pecked me on the tail. Scared the fool out of me just for a second. I snarled at her and made her squawk and flap her wings.

That's another thing about this job. Every day, every night you put your life on the line, and for what? A bunch of idiot birds that would just as soon peck you on the tail as tell you good morning. Sometimes you wonder if it's worth it, and all that keeps you going is dedication to duty.

In the end, that's what separates the top echelon of cowdogs from the common rubble . . . rabble, whatever the word is, anyway the dogs that don't give a rip, is what I'm saying.

Well, I had nothing to work with, no evidence, no case. There wasn't a thing I could do until the killer struck again. I could only hope that me and Drover could catch him in the act.

I decided to change my strategy. Instead of

throwing a guard around the chickenhouse, we would use the stake-out approach.

"Stake-out" is a technical term which we use in this business. Webster defines stake as "a length of wood or metal pointed at one end for driving into the ground." It comes from the Anglo-Saxon word *staca,* akin to the Danish *staak.*

"Out" is defined as "away from, forth from, or removed from a place, position, or situation." It comes from the Middle English *ut.*

That's about as technical as I can make it.

In layman's terms, a stake-out is basically a trap. You leave the chickenhouse unguarded, don't you see, and watch and wait and wait and watch until the villain makes his move, and then you swoop in and get him.

It's pretty simple, really, when you get used to the terminology.

At dark, me and Drover staked the place out. We hid in some tall weeds maybe thirty feet from the chickenhouse.

Time sure did drag. The first couple of hours we heard coyotes howling off in the pastures. Drover kept looking around with big eyes. I thought he might try to slip off to the machine shed, but he didn't. After a while, he laid his head down on his paws and went to sleep.

I could have kept him awake, I mean, pulled rank and *demanded* that he stay awake, but I thought, what the heck, the little guy probably needed the sleep. I figgered I could keep watch and wake him up when the time came for action.

Then I fell asleep, but the funny thing about it was that I dreamed I was awake, sitting here and standing guard. I kept saying, "Hank, are you still awake?" And Hank said, "Sure I am. If I was asleep, you and I wouldn't be talking like this, would we?" And I said, "No, I suppose not."

Seems to me it's kind of a waste of good sleep to dream about what you were doing when you were awake, but that's what happened.

I heard something squawk, and I said, "Hank, what's that?"

"Nuthin."

"You sure?"

"Sure I'm sure. You're wide awake and watching the stake-out, aren't you?"

"I think so, yes."

"Then stop worrying."

The squawking went on and the next thing I knew, Drover was jumping up and down. "Hank, oh Hank, he's back, murder, help, blood, we fell asleep, oh my gosh, Hank, wake up!''

"Huh? I ain't asleep.'' And right then my eyes popped open and I woke up. "Dang the luck, I *was* asleep! I was afraid of that.''

We dashed out of the weeds and found a body south of the chickenhouse door. The M.O. was the same. (There's another technical term, M.O. It stands for *Modus of Operationus,* which means *how it was done.* We shorten it to M.O.)

A pattern began to emerge. The killer had struck twice and both times he had killed a white leghorn hen. (Actually, that might not have been a crucial point because there weren't any other-colored hens on the place, but I mention it to demonstrate the kind of deep thinking that goes into solving a case of this type. You can't overlook a single detail, even those that don't mean anything.)

But the most revealing clue was that the murderer hadn't dragged his victim off. That meant that he hadn't killed for food, but only for the sport of it. In other words, we had a pathagorical killer on the loose.

This was very significant, the first big break in the case. At last I had an M.O. that narrowed the suspects down to coyotes, coons, skunks, badgers, foxes . . . rats, it hadn't eliminated anybody and I was right back where I started.

I hunkered down and studied the body. It was still warm. Warm chicken. My mouth began to water and I noticed a rumble in my stomach. This fresh evidence was pointing the case in an entirely new direction.

"Uh Drover, why don't you run on and get some sleep? You've had a tough day."

"Oh, I'm awake now."

"You look sleepy."

"I do?"

"Yes, you do, awful sleepy. Your eyes seem kind of baggy."

"Don't you think we should sound the alarm?"

"Not just yet. I need to do a little more study on the corpse." My stomach growled real loud.

Drover perked his ears. "What was that?"

"I didn't hear anything."

He waited and listened. I concentrated on making my stomach shut up. You can do that, you know, control your body with your mind, only it didn't work this time. My stomach growled again, sounded like a rusty gate hinge.

"What *is* that?"

"Rigor mortis," I said. "Chickens do that.

Run along now and get some sleep. We've got a big day ahead of us."

"Well, okay." He started off and heard my stomach again. He turned around and twisted his head and stared at me. "Was that *you*?"

"Don't be absurd. Good night, Drover."

He shrugged and went on down to the gas tanks. I gave him plenty of time to bed down, get comfortable, snap at a few mosquitoes, and fall asleep. My mouth was watering so much that it was dripping off my chin.

When everything was real quiet, I snatched up the body, loped out into the horse pasture, and began my post mortem investigation. It was very interesting.

I didn't hurry this part of the investigation. I labored over my work for several hours and fell into a peaceful sleep.

When I awoke it was bright daylight. I could feel the rays of the sun warming my coat. I glanced around, trying to remember where I was, and when I figured it out, my heart almost stopped beating.

I was lying in the center of a circle of white feathers, and several more feathers were clinging to my mouth and nose. My belly bulged, and Sally May was standing over me, a look of horror on her face.

"Hank! *You're* the one! Oh Hank, how could you!"

Huh? No wait, there had been a mistake. I had only . . . well, you see, I just . . . the chicken was already dead and I thought . . . hey, listen, I can explain everything . . .

It must have looked pretty bad, me lying there in the midst of all that damaging evidence. Sally May headed down to the house, swinging her arms and walking fast.

I didn't know what to do. If I ran, it would look bad. If I stayed, it would look bad. No matter what I did, it would look bad. Maybe eating the dern chicken had been a mistake.

I was still sitting there, mulling over my next course of action, when Sally May returned with her husband.

"There, look. You see who's been killing the chickens? *Your dog!*"

I whapped my tail against the ground and put on my most innocent face. Loper and I had been through a lot together. Surely he would know that his Head of Ranch Security wasn't a common chicken-killing dog. He had to trust me.

But I could see his face harden, and I knew I was cooked. "Hank, you bad dog. I never would have thought you'd do something like this."

I didn't! It was all a mistake, I'd been framed.

"Come here, Hank," I crawled over to him. He picked up the chicken head which was lying on the ground. I hadn't eaten it because I've found that beaks are hard to swaller. He tied a piece of string around the head and tied it around my neck. "There. You wear that chicken head until it falls off. Maybe that'll help you remember that killing hens doesn't pay around here."

They left, talking in low voices and shaking their heads. I tried to bite the string and get that thing off my neck, but I couldn't do it. I was feeling mighty low, mighty blue. I was ashamed of myself, but also outraged at the injustice of it.

I headed down to the corral to find Drover. Instead, I ran into Pete the barn cat, just the guy I didn't want to see. He was sunning himself in front of the saddle shed—in other words, *loafing,* which is what he does about ninety-five percent of the time. The mice were rampant down at the feed barn, but Pete couldn't work a mouse patrol into his busy schedule. It interfered with his loafing. That's a cat for you.

He saw me before I saw him. He yawned and a big grin spread across his mouth. "Nice necklace you got on, Hankie. Where could a feller buy one of those?"

You have to be in the mood for Pete, and I wasn't. I made a dive for him and he escaped instant death by a matter of inches. He hissed and ran, and I fell in right behind him.

I chased him around the corrals. He hissed and I barked. There were several horses in the

west lot and they all started bucking and kicking up their heels. It was my lousy luck that
Slim happened to be riding one of them—a
two-year-old colt, as I recall—and he started
yelling.

"Hank, get outa here! Whoa, Sinbad, easy
bronc!"

Nobody around here ever yells at the cat.
Why? I don't know, I just don't understand.

I gave up the chase. I would settle accounts
with Pete some other day. I loped over to the
gas tank, looking for Drover. He heard me
coming, sat up, saw the chicken head around
my neck, turned tail, and sprinted for the
machine shed as fast as he could go.

"Drover, wait, it's me, Hank!"

He kept going. I guess he didn't want to get
involved with a criminal.

I went down to the gas tank and lay down.
Boy, I felt low. I tried to sleep but didn't have
much luck. That chicken head was starting to
smell, and it reminded me all over again of the
injustice of my situation.

Off in the distance, I could hear Pete. He
was still up in the tree he had climbed to
escape my attack, and he was singing a song
called "Mommas, Don't Let Your Puppies
Grow Up to be Cowdogs." Now and then he

would stop singing, and I would hear him laughing. Really got under my skin.

I lay there brooding for a long time. Then I pushed myself up and all of a sudden it was clear what I would have to do. They had left me no choice.

I took one last look at my bedroom there under the gas tank, and started up the hill. As I passed by the machine shed door, Drover stuck his head out.

"Psst! Where you going?"

I trotted past. "I'm leaving."

He crept out, glanced around to see if anybody was watching, and came after me. "Leaving?"

"That's right. I quit, I resign."

His jaw dropped. "You can't do that."

"You just watch me. This chicken head was the last straw. I'm fed up with this place. I'm moving on."

"Moving . . . where you going?"

"I don't know yet. West, toward the setting sun."

He was quiet for a minute, then, "I'll go with you."

"No you won't."

"How come?"

"Because, Drover, I'm starting a new life.

I'm gonna become an outlaw."

The breath whistled through his throat. "An outlaw!"

"That's right. They've driven me to it. I tried to run this ranch, but it just didn't work. I'm going back to the wild. One of these days, they'll be sorry."

"But Hank . . ."

"Goodbye, Drover. Take care of things. I'm sorry it has to end this way. Next time we meet, I won't be Hank the Cowdog. I'll be Hank the Outlaw. So long."

And with that, I trotted off to a new life as a criminal, outcast, nomad, and wild dog.

CHAPTER

6

BUZZARDS

I made my way north, away from headquarters and up into the canyon country. If a dog was going to go back to the wild, that was the place to go.

Funny, how good it felt walking away from everything—the job, the responsibility, the constant worry. When I crossed the road there by the mailbox, I felt free for the first time in years.

On the other side of the road, I stopped and looked back. Drover had followed me about a hundred yards and stopped. He was watching. Maybe he thought I would change my mind and go back. Maybe he was waiting for me to tell him to come on.

I didn't. I ran my eyes over the ranch I had loved and protected for so many years, waved farewell to Drover, and went on my way.

I wondered how Loper and Slim and Sally May would react when they figgered out that I had resigned and moved on. I had an idea they'd be sorry. They'd realize how they'd done me wrong and misjudged me and accused me of terrible things I didn't do. I mean, all I did was eat a dead chicken, and she wasn't a bit deader when I finished than when I started.

Maybe they'd cry. Why not? A lot of people cry over their dogs. They tell me that when Lassie and Rin Tin Tin were big on TV, people used to cry when they thought Lassie was in a jam he couldn't get out of, and when Rinny had got himself chewed up by a bear and it appeared that he wouldn't pull out of it.

People never realize just how important a dog is until it's too late. In life we get yelled at and cursed and kicked around, but when we're gone, people wish they had us back.

Yeah, they'd cry when they found out that old Hank had moved on, and they'd cry even harder when it dawned on them that their ranch was being protected—and I mean so-called protected—by Pete the cat and Drover the chicken-hearted.

That would wring tears out of a bodark post.

Yep, they'd cry and they'd say, "Oh, I wish we had Hankie back! He had his faults but he was a good honest dog. It just won't be the same around here without him."

Around sundown, they'd walk out into the pasture and call, "Here Hank, come on Hankie, here boy!"

And you know what? I'd be up in them canyons, eating fresh meat instead of Co-op dog food, listening to the sounds of nature, and enjoying pure peace and freedom.

I'd hear 'em calling my name, begging me to come back, but I wouldn't go. They'd had their chance. I'd tried to go straight and live within the law but they'd drove me to drastic measures, drove me to follow the owl-hoot trail and become an outlaw.

Next morning, they'd get in the pickup and go driving around, checking all the spots where I used to hang out: the sewer, the gas tanks, the corral, the creek. But I wouldn't be there.

Then they'd drive over to the neighbor's place. "Anybody seen Hank? We've lost our cowdog. No? Well, we're offering a five hundred dollar reward to anybody who finds him."

Then they'd start driving through the pastures, honking the horn and calling, "Hank, here boy! Come on home, Hankie, we miss you. We're sorry for everything we've done. We'll do anything if you'll just come home."

Laying off in them canyons, I'd hear 'em calling. Peeking through the rocks, I'd see 'em driving slow across the pasture. But I wouldn't go back. Injustice had changed me, turned me bitter and snapped something inside me.

Anyway, that's what I was thinking about when I turned my back on the ranch forever and hit the owl-hoot trail.

They say you're not supposed to feel good about other people's misfortunes, but I got to admit that it gave me considerable wicked pleasure to know that I had left 'em weeping, and that with me gone the ranch was gonna fall apart real quick.

That's the kind of satisfaction that dog food and a flea collar just won't buy.

Must have been late afternoon when I reached the wild country, up near the head of one of them canyons. It was pretty hot down there, not much breeze. The canyon walls rose up a hundred feet in the air and a couple of buzzards floated in the sky overhead.

I was pretty tired and my feet was kind of sore from walking over the rocks, so when I found a little spring of water, I jumped in and rolled around. It was pleasant but not nearly as satisfying as a roll in the sewer.

That was one thing about my old life that I would miss. I always looked forward to the middle of the day when me and Drover used to go down to the place where the septic tank overflowed, hop in, and splash and roll around with our paws in the air and then get out and have a good old fashioned head-to-tail shake.

You can say what you want about spring water, but if you ask me, it ain't near as refreshing or healthful as good old septic tank water. And I always liked the deep rich manly smell of it. A dog ought to smell like a dog, seems to me, and I never had no desire to be one of those town dogs that get their hair clipped and their toenails painted and get sprayed all over with that stinking perfume stuff. Perfume gives me a headache and stops up my nose.

Anyway, that spring pool wasn't as refreshing as the sewer would have been, but I managed to cool myself down and satisfy my thirst. I wallered around in it for ten or fifteen minutes, and when I was ready to get out, I noticed that I had some company.

Those buzzards that had been floating around the rim of the canyon had dropped in for a visit, two of 'em. They were perched on the ground near the edge of the pool, staring at me.

I showed 'em some fangs right away. I mean, I try to be friendly and all of that, but there's just something about a buzzard that don't sit right with me. Maybe it's because they're so ugly. Looks ain't everything in this life, unless you happen to look like a turkey buzzard, and then they're pretty crucial. It's hard to be friendly to something that ugly.

I gave 'em a growl. They bent their necks forward and stared at me. Then Wallace, the older of the two, said, "We thought maybe you was dead."

"Thinking gets birds like you in trouble. Run along, I got things to do."

They didn't move, so I stepped out on dry land and shook myself. Throwed water all over Wallace. He dropped his wings and took a couple of steps backward.

"He ain't dead, Junior. You made a mistake."

"I tell you, he's d-d-dead, Pa, I just know he he he is." Junior seemed to have a little studder problem. "When I pick up a s-s-signal, something's du-du-du-dead. Remember that ground squirrel? I picked him up at five hundred y-y-yards, and what did *you* su-say?"

Wallace frowned and squinted one eye. "I don't recall. What did I say?"

"You su-su-said I was su-seeing things, seeing things. You said my eyes was h-h-h-hooked up to my b-b-b-b-b-b . . ."

"Belly, uh, huh, it's coming back now."

"And you s-s-said I didn't have enough ex perience and when I g-g-got as old as you, old as you, m-maybe I'd amount to s-s-something."

"I was just trying to be optimistic, son, you can't blame me for that." Wallace burped and the whole canyon went sour. "Dang, I'm hungry."

"I'm t-t-telling you, Pa, he's du-du-du-dead. I picked up the s-s-signals, signals."

They moved a little closer and looked me over real careful. "Junior, if he's dead, how come he crawled out of that water hole?"

"Bu-beats me."

"And how come his eyes are open and he's looking back at us?"

"Bu-beats me, but he's dead."

"Maybe so, son. I never claimed to know everything."

"You du-did too, yesterday m-m-morning."

"All right, all right, I take it back. Hey!" His head shot up in the air. "I'm starting to pick up the signals now. He *is* dead, you're right!"

"Told you s-s-so."

They came toward me. I watched 'em and lifted my lip on the right side.

"Whoa, Junior, hold it, son! Did you see that lip go up? Did you see them teeth? Look there, son, see what I'm saying?"

Junior stretched out his skinny neck and studied me for a minute. "That d-don't mean n-nuthin. I'll p-p-p-prove it, prove it."

And with that, Junior marched up and pecked me on top of the head. As you might imagine, I didn't care for that and I took a snap at Junior and relieved him of a double handful of feathers. The buzzards went running for cover. The old man tripped over a rock, went down, hopped up, and kept going, looking back over his wing the whole time.

"I told you he wasn't dead!"

"But Pa . . ."

"I told you once, I told you twice, I told you three times!"

"But Pa . . ."

"You're gonna keep fooling around and get us hurt one of these days."

"But Pa . . . what's that around his neck?"

"Huh?" They were back to looking at me again.

"That's where the s-s-signal's coming from, that thing around his n-n-n-n-n, under his chin."

Old Wallace's eyes popped open and a smile came over his beak. "I believe you're right, son. It's a chicken head!'' Wallace put on a pleasant face (for a buzzard) and came waddling over to me. "Hi there. You new around here?"

"Maybe."

"I'm Wallace, this here's Junior, and we was just . . . what would you take for that chicken head?"

"What you got?"

They went into a huddle, then the old man said, "Tell you what, neighbor, times are hard right now. My eyes is going bad on me and Junior's a little on the simple-minded side of things, and we haven't had a good meal in three days. We sure are hungry and we sure could use a chicken head right now, till our luck changes. We'd have to take it on credit, is the long and short of it."

"We'd d-do you a fu-fu-fu-favor sometime, sometime."

Wallace nodded his head. "Yes we would, we surely would, because we never forget a good deed."

I thought it over. Seemed to me that trading a stinking chicken head for a buzzard's good will was about an even swap. You couldn't take either one of them to the bank.

"Tell you what, boys, if you can chew the

string in half, I'll let you have the head."

Their eyes lit up and Junior started toward me, only the old man slapped him across the mouth with his wing. "I'll handle this. You just stand by for further orders."

Wallace waddled over and squinted at the string. He leaned out his neck and took a bite, got my ear instead of the string. I yelped and jumped away.

"I'm sorry, dang I'm sorry. It's my eyes. Let me try again."

"All right, try again, but leave the ear where it sits."

He tried again, and this time he found the string and chewed it in half. Just as soon as the head hit the ground, Junior made a dive for it, swooped it up in his beak, and ran off.

The old man went after him, flapping his wings and stumbling over rocks and things. "Junior, you come back here! Junior!"

They fought over it for five minutes. First Junior had it, then Wallace had it, then they got so busy fighting that it fell to the ground. A chicken hawk swooped down and picked it up, and that was the last they ever saw of their supper.

That stopped the fight. "See what you done!" Wallace squawked.

"*You* d-d-done it cause you're so g-g-greedy, greedy."

It was about dark by this time, so I found me a comfortable spot and curled up for the night. Junior and Wallace argued back and forth for another hour, until at last they shut up and we had some peace and quiet. I was drifting off to sleep when I heard Junior's voice.

"P-Pa?"

"What?"

"I'm h-hungry."

"You oughta be, after the way you acted." Silence. "P-Pa?"

"What!"

"You ever eat a d-d-dog?"

I raised my head. "The first son of a buck that comes creeping around me in the night is gonna get his legs tore off, one by one."

Didn't hear another sound out of them birds for the rest of the night, and they didn't stay for breakfast.

C H A P T E R

7

TRUE LOVE

A ctually there wasn't any breakfast. And then there wasn't any lunch. Along toward the middle of the afternoon, it occurred to me that if I wanted to eat, I would have to get out and hustle some grub.

I left camp and lit out north, figuring I would scout the head of the canyon. I hadn't gone very far when I stopped dead in my tracks. I heard something, kind of a clanking sound.

I slipped behind a bush and studied the country ahead. I kept hearing that sound but I couldn't see what was causing it. Then my sharp cowdog eyes picked up some movement.

At first glance it appeared to be a medium sized, bushy-tailed dog stumbling around without a head. Well, that didn't make sense. I'm not so easily fooled. My years of security work told me that there was more to this thing, so I decided to investigate.

A dog without a head? I didn't believe it.

I moved closer and pieced together the following details:

1) The subject wasn't a dog. He was a coyote, age approximately three years and five months, weight thirty-seven pounds, length (including tail) forty-three inches.

2) He was not a he. He was a *she,* meaning a female of the species, rather homely, as coyotes tend to be, but not without charm.

3) Subject had stuck her head into a Hawaiian Punch can with the top cut out. The can had lodged around her ears and gotten stuck there, leaving her blind and helpless.

One of the first rules you learn as a cowdog is that cowdogs and coyotes don't mix. They're natural enemies, the former devoted to protection of home, livestock, and civilization, the latter devoted to a dissolute style of life based on raiding, depredation, and uncivilized forms of behavior.

In other words, I had every reason to walk away and leave the coyote to her fate—a slow, lingering death. In this business you can't be sentimental.

Still, death inside a Hawaiian Punch can seemed too cruel even for a coyote. I just couldn't walk away and leave her to die, even though I had a feeling that if I helped her, I would regret it.

"Afternoon, ma'am. My name's Hank the Cowdog. Appears to me that you're in distress."

When she heard my voice, she bristled and tried to run away. Didn't go far, though, ran into a rock. She stopped, lay flat on the ground, and didn't move.

I recognized this as the natural sneaky reaction of the coyote breed. When you catch them red-handed, if they can't run away, they'll lie flat on the ground. I suppose they think they're blending into the surroundings. It's hard to say what they think. Coyotes are different.

"You don't need to be afraid, ma'am. I'm here to help you." She didn't say a word or move a muscle. "Lie still and I'll see if I can get that thing off your head."

I don't know how much of this she understood. Coyotes don't speak the same language

© G.L. Holmes
1982

as dogs, don't you see. Some of the words are similar and some aren't. Modern Doglish and the coyote dialect both come from the same linguistic root, which was the ancient language spoken by our common ancestors many years ago before the species split into *Dogus Domesticus* and *Dogus Coyotus.*

This is pretty technical stuff, and I don't want to bore anyone, but it's important that the reader understand these things.

Well, it just so happened that I was fluent in the coyote dialect, so I decided to address the lady in her own language.

"Me not hurt Missy Coyote. Me friend, me help Missy. Missy have trouble."

"You not hurt?" Her voice echoed inside the can.

"Me not hurt. Me help. Missy Coyote lie still, not move. Hank fixy real quick."

For a long time she didn't speak. Then, "Missy lie still."

It was important that I got the point across to her that I was a friend, don't you see, because it would have been typical coyote behavior for her to jump up, once I got the can off her head, and tear off one of my ears. They're just a little bit crazy, them coyotes, and you've got to be careful.

Anyway, she lay still while I hooked my front paws around the can and started pulling. I pulled and I tugged and I strained and I grunted, and finally the can popped free.

That's when I got my first look at Missy Coyote's face.

I'm not one to gush or be overwhelmed. Let's get that straight right here. My years in the security business have trained me to look upon most things as mere facts, facts to be gathered and studied and analyzed.

I mean, I'd seen women before, lots of 'em, scads of 'em. I'd been through times in my life when women were hanging all over me, and I literally couldn't take a step without bumping into an adoring female.

If you're a cowdog, you get used to this. It's common knowledge that cowdogs are just a little bit special. Read your dog books, ask anyone who knows about dogs, check it out with the experts. They'll tell you that women flip over cowdogs.

What I'm saying—and I'm just trying to put it all into perspective, don't you see—is that I wasn't one of these dogs that chased women all the time or even had much interest in them.

But you know what? When I seen Missy Coyote's face, with those big eyes and that fine tapered nose, I got weak in the legs and kind of swimmy in the head. She was the by George prettiest thang I'd ever laid eyes on.

"Missy Coyote . . . pretty."

She was still blinking her eyes against the glare of the sun. Guess she'd been in that can for a day or two. When she got used to the sunlight, she looked me over real close. Then she smiled.

I melted. I mean, I actually fell over and started kicking my legs in the air. It was an unconscious, unwanted response, not the kind of reaction you'd expect from a professional cowdog. But as I've pointed out before, I was only flesh and blood.

Missy didn't understand my spasm, I reckon, and she came over. Had her head cocked to the side like this—oh well, you can't see—she had her head cocked to the side.

"What wrong? You sick?"

"Yeah, I'm sick all right. I need to get out of here." I struggled to my feet and tried to leave, but my back legs didn't function.

"Not leave," she said. "Stay. Tell name."

I was sure she could hear my heart beating. I could. It was about to take off the top of my head, to be exact. "Me Hank," I finally managed to say.

Her eyes brightened. "Pretty name, Hunk."

"Not Hunk. *Hank.*"

She nodded. "Yes, Hunk. Pretty name. Me like. Hunk."

"Whatever you say."

"Me called Girl-Who-Drink-Blood."

"Girl-Who-Drink-Blood!"

She nodded and smiled. "You like?"

There wasn't a whole lot of poetry in that name, seemed to me. Her old lady, or whoever named her, must have been a real barbarian.

"Me no like. Me call you Missy Coyote. Like Missy Coyote moreso. Bloody name not pretty."

She laughed. "Bloody name pretty to co-yote. Coyote like blood. Make grow strong, keep hair pretty in winter. Hunk no like blood in winter?"

"Hank eat Co-op dog food in winter, no need blood."

"What means, Co-op dog food?"

"No can explain. Too complicated."

"Why Hunk here, not at people-place with many building and house with chicken?"

"Hank get mad at people, quit job. People no understand. Hank no more guard chicken. Hank follow outlaw trail."

Her eyes widened. "Outlaw trail dangerous. Live out in wild, coyote around. Coyote not like Hunk."

I decided it was time to turn on some of my charm, just a little at a time. Didn't want to give the girl the full load all at once. "Missy Coyote like Hank?"

She smiled. Mercy! Made me weak in the legs again. "Missy think Hunk cute."

"Ah heck, really? Me cute?"

Her smile faded. "But other coyote not think so. Missy have brother named Scraunch. Not like ranch dog, hurt if find."

"*You're* Scraunch's sister?"

She nodded. I knew about Scraunch, the most notorious outlaw coyote in the whole country. He was big, mean, and utterly heartless. He'd probably killed more chickens and barn cats than any three coyotes on the ranch, and it was common knowledge that he'd kill a stray dog just for the sport of it.

As a matter of fact, me and Scraunch had met on the field of battle and had fought to a draw—which I had considered a victory. That was back in the winter. January, as I recall, yes it was, because we fought in the snow. Scraunch was a real thug.

"How can a nice girl like you have such a bad brother?"

She shook her head. "Hunk be careful, maybe go back ranch. Not safe here."

I leaned forward and nuzzled her under the chin with the end of my nose. "I ain't scared. Hank ready to fight whole family for Missy."

I noticed that she started trembling, thought maybe it was the result of my charm. Then she whispered, "Hunk in trouble. Whole family here."

"Huh?"

I looked around. She wasn't kidding. The whole danged family had arrived. We was surrounded by lean-limbed, long-haired, scruffy-tailed, yellow-eyed, slack-jawed, hungry-looking coyotes.

I was in trouble, fellers, and had a feeling that a wreck was coming.

CHAPTER
8

HANK RUNS A BLUFF

Missy's old man was the chief. His full proper name was Many-Rabbit-Gut-Eat-In-Full-Moon, which in coyote culture was regarded as a beautiful name. Can you imagine a mother saddling an innocent pup with a name like that? Shows just how backward them coyotes were.

Anyway, nobody used his full name except at rituals and war councils and such. Mostly they called him Chief Gut or just plain Gut.

Gut was an old devil, skinny. You could count every rib he owned on both sides. Looked like a one-way plow with a wet blanket throwed over the discs. Walked with a limp, packed his right front leg which was missing a couple of toes. Had a long scar down the front of his face, nose was all beat up, and his left ear looked as though the rats had been chewing on it.

He came limping over to where I was and, strangely enough, he had a smile on his face. Made me feel a little better about things.

"Ah ha," he laughed, "daughter catch dog! Coyote girl pretty, huh?"

"Mighty pretty, yes she is."

"You like, huh?" He turned to the other coyotes. "Dog like Girl-Who-Drink-Blood. Think she pretty." They roared at that, got a good chuckle out of it. I must have missed the joke. Old Gut turned back to me. "Oh foolish dog to chase coyote girl into canyon. Berry berry foolish you leave ranch, come here without big-hat and boom-boom."

I'm doing my best to translate this conversation from the coyote dialect, but maybe I ought to pause here to clear up some of the terminology.

Big-hat was the coyote word for cowboy, and *boom-boom* meant gun. Thought I better get that straight. I mean, you can't expect everyone to be fluent in three or four or five languages. I was, but that was just part of my job, one of the many things a top-notch cowdog had to master before he could take over a ranch and run it the way it ought to be run.

I might also mention that I had a fair knowledge of the coon, possum, and badger dialects, and I could bluff my way through in chicken and prairie dog. Actually, chicken is pretty simple. Chickens are so dumb that they only have about half a dozen words in the whole language, and three of those words are just different ways of saying *help*!

All right, we've got that out of the way. Now, where was I? Old Gut turned to me. "Oh foolish dog to chase coyote girl into canyon. Berry . . ." We've already heard that. "Now you in big trouble, ha! You do good job, Daughter, catch dog."

"Not catch dog," she said. "Dog help, save life. Name Hunk. Hunk friend."

The old man scowled. "Hunk not friend. Fight coyote many time away from chicken. He chicken dog."

Chicken dog. Them was fightin' words. If Missy hadn't been there to hold me back, I might have cleaned house on the whole coyote nation. Me and old man Gut went nose to nose and were growling at each other when I caught some motion out of the corner of my eye. I looked. It was Scraunch.

He was crouched low, walking real slow. Hair along his backbone was bristled all the

G. L. Holmes
© 1982

way from the back of his neck to the tip of his tail. Had a snarl on his mouth that showed two rows of long white fangs. He was a big dude, tall, brawny, raw-boned, and so ugly that a guy could hardly stand to look him in the face. Kind of throwed a chill in me.

Old man Gut backed off. "Now what you say, Chicken Dog? You scared betcha, huh?"

I swallered and tried to keep my knees from going out on me. "Naw, I ain't scared."

"You not scared Scraunch, you not smart.

Scraunch berry bad fellow.''

I glanced at Missy. ''Tell your brother that I don't like the look on his face.''

She told him. He stopped and a roar of laughter went up from the other coyotes. When they quit yipping and howling, I went on. ''Tell your brother that if he takes one more step, I'm gonna use him to sweep this whole pasture, and when I get done, there won't be a cactus bush left in Ochiltree County.''

She told him. He grinned and took another step.

''Tell your brother that I saw that, and I won't forget it.''

Missy shook her head. ''Not talk so big. Make Scraunch mad. Big mouth make big trouble.''

One of the first rules you learn in security work is an old piece of dog wisdom: never bite if you can bark; never bark if you can growl; never growl if you can talk; and never talk if you can run.

In other words, when the odds are against you, the best kind of fight is none at all. That was my strategy, see. The longer I talked, the longer I could stay alive. And who knows, I just might say something that would change

Scraunch's mind about tearing me limb from limb, though I didn't have a great deal of hope.

He was standing maybe four, five feet in front of me. A hush had fallen over the tribe and all eyes were on the two of us. He sat down and leered at me. And I mean *leered,* brother. That wasn't no ordinary grin.

I leered right back, tried to anyway, though I'd never really perfected a good leer. Then I turned to Missy again.

"Tell your brother that I've changed my mind. If he can mind his manners and act right, we'll forget the whole thing."

Missy started to speak, but Scraunch lifted his paw for silence. "Not speak through sister," he said in a deep rumbling voice. "You have talk, you speak Scraunch."

"All right," I nodded, "you asked for it, you've really done it this time. I was prepared to forget the whole thing and just let it slide, but by George if you're going to keep pushing and mouthing off, well hey, this could get serious. Come on."

He didn't move.

"*Come on!* Get off your duff and let's settle this thing once and for all. I'm tired of waiting. I mean, I came out here to get *you,* Scraunch. Oh, I know, you thought I was messing around with your sister. Ha! That's just what I wanted you to think. It was a trap, Scraunch, and you walked right into it.

"Oh, what a dumb brute you are! I didn't think you'd actually fall for it. I never dreamed it would be this easy. All these months I've been waiting to even the score between us, and I never dreamed I could just walk into the canyon and you'd come to me!"

Speaking of silence, them coyotes was silent. Guess they couldn't believe what they were hearing. Scraunch glanced at Chief Gut and Gut glanced at Missy and Missy glanced at me, and I gave her a smile and a wink.

Scraunch stood up, and so did the hair on the back of his neck. "Scraunch kill chicken dog."

"You think so? *You actually think that?*" I cut loose with a wild laugh. "Holy cats, where have you been all your life? You've been up in the bojacks too long, Scraunch, you're so country it hurts. I mean, you're pathetic. I almost feel sorry for you." I took a step toward him. "You still don't understand, do you? It still hasn't soaked through your thick barbarian skull that you've walked right into my trap. Ho, I can't believe this!"

Scraunch cut his eyes toward old Gut.

"Scraunch kill chicken dog." But there was a little less conviction this time.

"Okay." I marched right up to him, until there weren't more than a couple of inches between our noses. "If you're bound and determined to go through with this, let's get it on. But first, I want you to do something. I want you to ask yourself this question: Why would a smart dog walk right into the middle of a bunch of coyotes, in *their* country? Put your little brain to work on that, Scraunch. If you figger it out, you'll know the secret. I'll give you thirty seconds."

Nobody moved. There wasn't a sound, not a whisper. Fifteen seconds went by *real* slow. I was in the process of checking out the escape routes when an old woman coyote (Scraunch's mother, it turned out) broke the circle and came out to him. She whispered something in his ear.

"No!" he growled. "Scraunch not scared, kill chicken dog!"

The old lady went to whispering again, then old Chief Gut limped over and joined the conference. It was kind of agitated. They growled and snapped and snarled—typical coyote family discussion, I would imagine.

"All right," I yelled, "time's up. I'm out of

patience. Have you figgered out the secret or shall we start spilling blood?''

The old lady led Scraunch away. He glared daggers at me over his shoulder. Old Chief Gut came over and stood in front of me.

"Not fight today."

"Rats," I said, and almost fainted with relief. "All right, if that's the way you want it. We'll let it slide this time, but I'm warning you, don't ever let this happen again."

"Not happen again."

"Good. I guess we understand each other."

"We understand."

"Very good. Now, if you coyotes will just stay where you are, I'll slip out of here and get on my way." I started backing away and ran into three big coyote bucks. "Scuse me, boys, if you'll just . . .''

"Hunk not understand." Missy came over. "Hunk stay, become coyote warrior, prove himself many fight and marry Missy Coyote."

"*HUH?*"

I shot a glance at Chief Gut, who was grinning and bobbing his head. "Yes, berry good you stay. Make outlaw, make warrior."

"Make warrior? Well, I . . . I've always wanted . . . but I really have to . . .'' I tried to ease around the three coyotes who were blocking my path. When I moved, they moved. They didn't intend to let me out of there, is the way it looked.

"Stay, not leave," the chief went on. "Old coyote tradition, adopt brave dog, make brother."

"Brave? Well, I can set you straight on that. You see . . ."

"Together we kill many chicken, eat cat every day, howl at moon, oh boy."

"I don't know about eating cat. I never . . ." I tried again to edge around those three bruisers, but they pushed me back.

"*Dog not leave,*" said the Chief.

"Yes sir."

"Maybe later marry daughter, have many pup. Everybody happy but Scraunch. Too bad. He not understand secret."

There was no chance of me getting out of there, so I walked over to the chief. "You figgered out the secret?"

He laughed and nodded his head. "Oh yes, berry much."

"What did you figger out?"

Gut glanced over his shoulders and brought his mouth right next to my ear. "Secret too secret to tell."

"You got it, all right, you sure did."

We had a good laugh, me and Old Gut, but I doubt that we were laughing about the same thing.

CHAPTER

9

ME JUST A WORTHLESS COYOTE

That business about the secret was the perfect stroke, and it probably saved my life. In desperation, I had lucked into it. Turns out that coyotes are superstitious animals, even though they're known to be cunning and vijalent vijalunt vijallunt vijjullunt . . .

I don't know how to spell that word. Spelling is a pain in the neck. I do my best with it, but I figger if a guy has tremendous gifts as a writer, his audience will forgive a few slip-ups in the spelling department.

I mean, it doesn't take any brains to open a dickshunary and look up a word. Anybody can do that. The real test of a writer comes in the creative process. I try to attend to the big picture, don't you see, and let the spelling take care of itself.

Vidgalent. Vidgallunt. Still doesn't look right.

Anyway, coyotes are superstitious brutes, and that deal about the secret caught them just right and saved my hide. Actually, it did better than that. It made me a kind of celebrity in the tribe, and I was treated like a visiting dignutarry digneterry dignitary, who cares?

By everyone but Scraunch, that is, and he continued to give me hateful glances and mutter under his breath every time our paths crossed. I couldn't blame him for being sore. I had won and he had lost, and you can't expect everyone to be a good loser. As we say in the security business, show me a good loser and I'll show you a loser.

Scraunch had lost a big one, and I was confident that he would hate my guts forevermore, even though there was a good chance that I would eventually become his brother-in-law.

You know, when Missy had first mentioned that possibility, it hadn't struck me as a real good idea. I suppose at that time I was still thinking of going back home, back to Drover and Pete, the chickens, the sewer, the cowboys, my old job. But a couple of days in the coyote village pretty muchly convinced me that I had found my true place in the world—as a savage.

The life of a savage ain't too bad. I admit that I was raised with a natural prejjudise predguduss *bias* against coyotes. Ma always told us that they were lazy, sneaky, undisciplined, and didn't have any ambition. But what chapped her most about coyotes was that they ate rotten meat and it made them smell bad.

True, every word of it. But what she *didn't* tell us was that laziness and riotous living can be a lot of fun. I don't blame her for not telling us that. I mean, she was trying to raise a litter of registered, papered, blue-ribbon, top-of-the-line cowdogs, and there's no better way to mess up a good cowdog than to let him discover that goofing off beats the heck out of hard work.

I discovered it by accident, and once I had a taste of indolence, I loved it. I mean, all at once I had no responsibilities, no cares, no worries. When I woke up in the morning, I didn't have to wonder if my ranch had made it through another night, or if I would get yelled at again for something I hadn't done.

About a week after I joined the tribe, I made friends with two brothers named Rip and

Snort. They were what you'd call typical good-old-boy coyotes: filthy, smelled awful, not real smart, loved to fight and have a good time, and had no more ambition than a couple of fence posts.

If Rip and Snort took a shine to you, you had two of the best friends in the world. If they didn't happen to like your looks or your attitude, you were in a world of trouble. I got along with them.

One evening along toward sunset, they came around and asked if I wanted to go carousing. I was feeling refreshed, since I'd slept a good part of the day—got up around noon and ate a piece of a rabbit that Missy had caught, then went back to bed. I was all rested up and said, "Sure I'd love to go carousing."

So off we went, me and Rip and Snort, on a big adventure. We went down the canyon, crossed that big sandy draw that cuts through there, then on across some rolling country until we came to an old silage pit. I'd been by it many times, but I'd never taken the time to go into the pit and check things out. By the time I took over the ranch, the cowboys had quit feeding silage, so I didn't know much about it.

One of the things I didn't know about silage was that it's fermented, which means that it's got some alkyhall in it, which means that if a guy eats enough of it, his attitude about the world will begin to change.

All those years I'd spent on the ranch, and I never knew any of that. But Rip and Snort knew all about silage, yes they did, and they had made a well-packed trail into and out of the silage pit.

So we started eating silage. Struck me as kind of bitter at first, but the more I ate the less I noticed the bitterness. By George, after about an hour of that, I thought it was as sweet as honey.

Well, we ate and we laughed and we laughed and we ate, and when it came time to leave, Rip and Snort had to drag me out of there, fellers, cause I just couldn't get enough of that fine stuff.

A big moon was out and we went single file down a cow path, Snort in the lead, me in the middle, and Rip on the caboose. Funny thing, that cow path kept wiggling around and I had a devil of a time trying to stay on it. I asked Rip about it and he said he was having the same trouble, derned path kept jumping from side to side. (I suspect the silage had something to do with it, is what I suspect.)

Well, next thing I knew, Snort topped a rise

© G.L.Holmes
1982

and came to a sudden halt, which caused a little pile-up, with me running into Snort and Rip running into me because couldn't any of us see real well at that point.

"Stop here," said Snort, "sing many song. Sing pretty, sing loud, teach Hunk coyote song."

So we all sat down on our haunches, throwed back our heads, and started singing. Let's see if I can remember how that song went.

"Me just a worthless coyote, me howling
at the moon.

Me like to sing and holler, me crazy
as a loon.

Me not want job or duties, no church or
Sunday school.

Me just a worthless coyote . . ." and I don't remember the last part, only it rhymed with "school." Pool or drool, something like that.

It was a crackerjack of a song. We ripped through it a couple of times, until I had her down. Then we divided up. Snort took the bass, Rip carried the melody, and I got up on the high tenor.

Don't know as I ever heard better singing. It was one of them priceless moments in life when three very gifted guys come together and blend their talents and sort of raise the cultural standards of the whole danged world. I mean, it was that good.

We sang it four or five times, then all at once Snort's ears perked up and he lifted his paw. We stopped and listened. Off in the distance, we heard yapping. There was something familiar about that yap, but for a minute I couldn't place it. Then it occurred to me that we were sitting on a spot just a quarter mile north of ranch headquarters.

That yapping was coming from Drover.

I think Rip and Snort had took a notion to amble on down there and see if they could get into a fight. I had to explain that they couldn't run fast enough to get Drover into a fight, that it would be a waste of their time.

"Let me go down and talk to him," I said. "He's an old buddy of mine. We used to work together. Maybe he'll come back and sing with us. We could use another guy on baritone."

They shrugged. Snort sat down and started scratching his ear. "More fun fight, but singing okay too. We wait."

So I trotted down to the ranch, weaving a little bit from side to side and humming "Me Just a Worthless Coyote." Say, that was a good song!

When I was, oh, twenty, twenty-five yards away, I slowed to a walk. I could see Drover up ahead of me. He was peering off in the distance. The little dope hadn't even seen me. I decided to stop and watch him for a minute.

He was all bunched up and tense. Off in the distance he could hear Rip and Snort laughing and belching and having a good time. He'd cock his head and listen for a minute, then he'd give out a yip-yip-yip. On every yip, all four feet went off the ground. Then he'd stop and listen again.

He never saw me, never had the slightest notion that I was sitting ten yards away from him, watching the whole show. This was my replacement, understand, the guy who had taken over my job as Head of Ranch Security. I didn't need anyone to tell me that the ranch had gone completely and absolutely to pot.

I cleared my throat. Drover froze. "What was that? Who's there?"

"What's going on, son?"

He gave out his usual squeak and in a flash he was high-balling it for the machine shed, squalling like a turpentined cat. He'd gone maybe ten, twelve yards when he slowed to a walk, then stopped.

"Hank, is that you?"

"Uh huh."

"It is?"

"Uh huh."

"How can I be sure? I thought you'd left the country."

"Well, why don't you just trot your little self over here and see."

He came real slow, a few steps at a time. "It . . . it sure sounds like you."

"Son of a gun."

"You're not fooling me, are you Hank?"

"Get over here and quit messing around."

"Okay, okay, I just . . . I want to be sure, that's all." He came creeping up to me. "Hank?"

"Boo."

He screamed and jumped straight up into the air. "Hank, stop that, don't do that to me! My nerves . . ."

"Drover, you ought to be ashamed of yourself. What a pitiful excuse you are for a night watchman. I could have carried off half the chickenhouse and you never would have gotten the news."

He hung his head. "I know it. I'm a failure. Every morning I wake up and say, 'Here's another day for you to mess up, Drover.' And I do, every one of them. It hasn't been the same since you left, Hank."

"I knew it wouldn't. I tried to tell 'em but they wouldn't listen. I mean, you can't treat a good dog like a dog and expect to keep him."

"Gosh, I wish you'd come back."

I laughed. "You can forget that, son, cause it'll never happen. I've found a better life."

He looked me over real careful. "What's come over you, Hank? You look different. You smell different. You *stink*."

"I've joined the coyote tribe."

I heard him gasp. "No!"

"That's right, and if you had a brain in your head, you'd come along and join up with 'em too. It ain't a bad life, let me tell you."

He took a couple of steps back. "I can't believe it. What would your mother say?"

"She'd say I was a turncoat and a traitor. So what? I tried the straight life, I did my job, and what did I get? Abuse. Ingratitude. No thanks, life's too short for that. I'll cast my lot with the outlaws of the world."

"Three weeks ago," he said in a quavery voice, "you were on the side of law and order, trying to catch the murderers. Now you're one of them."

"That's right."

He started crying. "Oh Hank, I can't take this! I used to admire you so much. You were my hero, I thought you were the greatest dog in the world. Since I was a pup, I just wanted to be like you, brave and strong and fearless . . ."

"Knock it off, Drover, I don't want to hear that stuff."

". . . and dedicated to duty. I knew I could never be as good as you, but I wanted to try. You were my idol, Hank."

"Cut it out, would you?"

"Come back home, Hankie. I need you. The ranch needs you. We all need you."

That kind of struck me in the heart, hearing Drover say those things. Then Rip and Snort called for me.

"Hunk! Come, sing. We tired wait!"

"Who's that?" Drover whispered.

"Oh, some of my pals. Come on up the hill with me, Drover, and I'll show you a good time, introduce you to my friends."

"Are they *drunk* like you?"

There was a little edge in his voice. He'd never talked to me like that before. "Well uh, maybe they are and maybe they ain't. Who cares?"

"I care. I don't associate with coyote trash."

"Well, lah-tee-dah! Aren't we high and mighty tonight."

Drover dried his eyes with the back of his paw. "I better get on back to the ranch. I'm on guard tonight."

I laughed in his face. "You're on guard! Son, you're a sorry excuse for a guard dog, running for the machine shed every time you hear a sound.''

"I'm not going to run any more, Hank. Somebody's got to protect the ranch. We can't depend on you any more.''

"You'll run. You always have, you always will.''

"I ain't going to run.''

"Sure you will, and I can prove it. *BOO!*'' He didn't run. "That don't prove a thing. When the time comes, when the chips are down, you'll run and hide.''

He looked me in the eye. "No I won't. And Hank, if you come with them, I won't run from you either.'' He turned and started walking away.

"You always were a little chump.''

He stopped. "I may be a chump, Hank, but I'm not a traitor. Goodbye.''

"Go on, you little dummy, who needs you anyway! Sawed-off, stub-tailed, self-righteous little pipsqueak!''

Drover went his way and I went mine. On my way up the hill, I could hear the boys singing "Me Just a Worthless Coyote" again. I took my place between Rip and Snort and started belting out the high tenor. We went on like that all night long, singing and laughing and chasing mice.

But it wasn't quite as much fun this time.

CHAPTER
10
AGED MUTTON

Must have been a couple of days later that I was sitting on the edge of the cap-rock, sunning myself and looking off in the distance. I'd been there most of the day, thinking about things and enjoying the quiet.

The coyote village was awful noisy. Seemed that somebody was always in the midst of a squabble. When a husband and wife had a difference of opinion, they just by George had a knock-down drag-out fight, right there in front of everybody. Nobody ever seemed to get hurt in these brawls, and I guess they managed to solve their problems, but I could never get used to the noise of it.

And the hair. After one of them family fights, the air was full of fur. A guy could hardly breathe for the hair.

And then there was the kids. There must have been ten or twelve pups in the village, and let me tell you about coyote pups.

Now, a *dog* pup is kind of cute. I'm not real fond of babies, understand, but even I have to admit that a little old cowdog pup is pretty cute. He'll be fat as a butterball and covered with silky hair, and when he looks up at you with those big soft eyes, you can't help but smile and say, "How's it going, kid?"

Coyote pups ain't cute. They look mean, they sound mean, they act mean, and fellers, they *are* mean. They've got two jaws-ful of teeth that are as sharp as needles, and their idea of good clean fun is to slip up behind some unsuspecting somebody (me, for instance) and just bite the heck out of his tail.

As a rule, I'm a pretty good sport. I was a kid once myself and I got into my share of mischief, but I can't get used to people biting my tail. I mean, there's something kind of special and private about a guy's tail. If he's got any pride at all, he tries to keep it nice, and he's a little fussy about scabs and bald spots and tooth marks and slobber and all that stuff.

What I'm saying is that my tail ain't a play toy.

But these kids, they'd sneak up behind me

and sink their little needle teeth into my tail. First few times, I just growled at 'em: "Here! Y'all go on, get out of here!" Didn't work. Coyotes are a little slow about taking a hint.

They came back and did it again, so I took sterner measures—cuffed one of 'em. Know what he did then? He *bit* me on the paw. Well, I wasn't going to take that off a dern kid, so I bit him on the scruff of the neck, and he somehow worked his way around and got hold of my left ear.

That got me all inflamed, don't you see, and I put the boy on the ground and was spanking some manners into him when his momma walked up.

"*You brute,* leave my Junior alone!"

"Huh?"

I looked around just in time to get slapped across the mouth. "There, bully!"

I suppose I shouldn't have slapped her back. But I did. *Whop,* right across the nose. "Maybe you can teach that boy some manners."

Whop! "Chicken dog!"

Whop! "Wild hag!"

She burst into tears and went bawling to her husband saying I was just an animal and had beat up her danged kid and called her a wild hag. Turned out she was Scraunch's woman, and here he came, all humped up and hair raised and yellow eyes aflaming.

I had taken about all I wanted off Scraunch and his family, and I was ready to go into combat, but Missy and her father jumped in between us and averted a civil war.

But the incident didn't do much to improve relations between me and Missy's brother. I had a feeling that sooner or later we were going to have a showdown.

Funny thing about all this. Them coyotes didn't mind chewing on each other. I mean, they were fighting all the time. But when *I* tried it, they didn't like it. Made me think that no matter how long I stayed there, they would always think of me as an outsider.

Anyway, I was sitting on the ledge, off to myself and away from the noise, when Missy came up behind me. She nuzzled me with her nose and ran her claws down my backbone. She knew I liked that.

"Something wrong? Hunk look sad."

"Oh, it's nothing. Just wanted to be alone, I guess."

"Not enjoy other coyote?"

"Well . . . do you ever get tired of all the noise, all that fighting and yelling?"

She shook her head. "That happy sound.

When coyote happy, make bunch noise. When we married, we happy, make bunch noise too."

"I see, yes, well, I guess we have that to look forward to, don't we?"

"When pup come, even more noise, oh boy."

"Oh boy."

"Hunk not be sad. Missy have something make Hunk feel good. We have feast, special food just for Hunk."

I followed her into the village. We went to her parents' den. They were sitting out in front and the old lady was pulling cockleburs out of the chief's tail. Missy asked her mother if she would prepare a special meal, just for me. She said she would. She left and was gone for ten, fifteen minutes.

I tried to make conversation with the old man but it wasn't easy. He started talking about the old days, about a time when he went a couple of rounds with a skunk. He seemed to think this story was hilarious. I thought it was moderately funny.

The chief was still cackling at his own wonderful story when the old lady returned, dragging in some horrible stinking something or other.

© G.L. Holmes
1982

I turned to Missy. "What's that?"

"Aged mutton."

"Aged mutton?"

She nodded and smiled. "Special feast make Hunk forget sadness."

Aged mutton. No doubt it had been buried for a while. It was green, dotted here and there with white spots which turned out to be maggots. The smell alone could have taken the paint off a corral fence. The taste of such rot was too horrible to imagine.

The old lady dragged it up and dropped it right at my feet. When she smiled at me, she looked an awful lot like her daughter, except she had several teeth missing and some of that green stuff hanging from her lower lip.

"Meat age for many month, just right for Hunk now."

The old man threw back his head, let out a howl, and dived into it. The old lady did the same. Missy did the same. I took a deep breath, said a little prayer, and dove in too.

Let's don't go into any details. It was bad. It was so bad that there are no words to describe it. I'll say no more.

An hour later, I was lying down, with my head over a cliff. I had emptied my body of everything but blood and a few bones. Missy stood over me, stroking my brow. She had been very nice about it. They all had been, even my future mother-in-law. She had decided that I had drunk some brackish water and that's what had made me sick.

"Hunk feel better now?"

"Feel better, sort of."

"Hunk like coyote feast, oh boy?"

"Oh boy."

"Now Hunk make ready for big raid?"

I raised up my head. "Huh?"

That was the first I had heard about the raid. This was going to be my big chance to prove to Missy's ma and pa that I was worthy of their daughter.

Scraunch was putting the deal together, a raid on the ranch.

CHAPTER

11

THE ATTACK ON
THE RANCH

Along about dark the coyote village came
to life. Everybody was excited.

"Fresh chicken, fresh cat!" they shouted.
"Oh boy!"

Even the kids were excited. They chased
each other around, practiced howling, and
played a game called "Get the Dog." The idea
of the game was that two kids played coyotes
and one played the guard dog. The coyotes
lured the dog out into a fight and then jumped
him.

I had played that game myself, only when
I'd played it it hadn't been a game, and I'd
been on the dog side. I'd never thought it was
much fun either.

After the sun went down, Scraunch climbed

up on a pile of rocks and gave a speech to the whole village. He was a firebrand and a rubble-rouser, and he preached the kind of hot gospel them coyotes wanted to hear.

"Jackrabbit run too fast, make coyote tired to catch. Mouse run down hole, coyote have to dig, make tired too. But *chicken* . . . chicken easy! Chicken nice and fat, sit on nest, not fight. Chicken plump and juicy. This night, everybody eat chicken!"

A cheer went up from the crowd. I was standing beside Missy, and she whooped and hollered along with the rest of them.

Scraunch waited for the cheering to die down and glanced over at me. "Ranch not have big guard dog now, only little white dog with cut-off tail. Maybe this night we kill dog too."

Another cheer went up. Scraunch watched me with a half-smile on his face. When I didn't cheer with the rest of them, he said, "What you say, Hunk? Maybe you help kill little white dog, huh?"

"Maybe so, Scraunch, maybe so."

Then he led the crowd in singing, "Me Just a Worthless Coyote," which was everybody's favorite song and sort of the coyote national anthem. I noticed that it brought tears to old

Chief Gut's eyes. Guess it brought back memories of his younger days.

When the song started, Rip and Snort came over to where I was and wanted to harmonize, just the way we did the night we went carousing. I tried but didn't feel much like singing.

But Rip and Snort bellered and howled and had themselves a big time. They were all excited about the raid, and they got into an argument over which one was going to give Drover the worst whipping. Listening to them snarl at each other, I got a funny feeling about good old boys. They have a way of changing into *mean* old boys and pretty quick.

The singing stopped and it was time to start the raid. Scraunch led the whole village in a howl, then those of us who were going on the raid lined up in a single file. Missy came over to tell me goodbye.

"Hunk have good fight, bring back fat chicken, prove to everybody that he good coyote."

"Thanks, Missy, I'll do my best."

"Then we marry, have seven-eight little pup."

"Seven or eight?"

She gave a yip and a howl. "Maybe nine-ten, oh boy!"

She nuzzled me under the chin, stepped

back, and gave me a smile. Geeze, she had a pretty face, but you know what? When she smiled, I saw her mother's face and remembered that aged mutton. It derned near ruined the occasion for me.

Scraunch came down the line, checking things out and giving orders to the men. When he came to me, he gave me a hard look.

"Better not make mistake. Scraunch watch close."

"You do that, Scraunch. You might learn something."

He gave me a sneer and went back to the front. With the rest of the village cheering, we marched down the canyon rim in a trot.

Once we left the village, Scraunch passed the order for silence. Down in the valley we got on a cow trail and followed it south toward the creek.

I couldn't help wondering where Drover was and what he was doing right now. Had he heard the singing? Did he run to the machine shed or was he out on patrol? I hoped, for his sake, that he was in the backest corner of the shed, cause these coyotes were in a dangerous mood.

As we slipped along through the night, I started putting a few things together. It was pretty clear by this time that Scraunch was the one who had been responsible for the chicken murders. He'd been slipping down there by himself and killing one or two a night, and now he'd decided to launch a full-scale invasion and share the spoils of war with the rest of the coyotes.

Funny, I'd solved the case, only now I was working for the other side. Life sure does play tricks on a guy, makes it awful hard to plan for the future. Growing up, I never would have dreamed that I'd end up a chicken-killer. I was kind of glad Ma wasn't around to see it.

About two hundred yards north of the ranch, Scraunch called a halt and gave the final orders for the attack. He told Rip and Snort to circle around and come in from the south, and sent another couple of guys over to the west.

He hadn't given me any orders, and that was good. I figgered I could lay low, stay out of the way, and show up when all the dust cleared.

"*You.*"

I looked around. "Huh?"

"You go with Scraunch. We get little white dog. Find out how bad you want sister."

"Well uh, surely I don't deserve such an honor."

"Not talk, only fight."

The others left, and me and Scraunch started sneaking toward the ranch. I felt sick. Things had gotten out of control. I hadn't wanted it to happen this way, me against my old buddy Drover. In his own bungling way, Drover was a nice dog. We'd had our squabbles and differences, but we'd had some good times too.

About twenty-five yards out, Scraunch stopped and dropped down into the grass. I squinted into the darkness and saw Drover standing beside the northeast corner of the machine shed. Just as you might expect, he wasn't looking in our direction. The little runt had no idea what was fixing to break loose.

A laugh growled in Scraunch's throat. "This easy. Dog stupid."

I couldn't argue with him. Facts is facts.

We crawled forward another ten, fifteen yards. Then, off to the south, Rip and Snort raised a howl. Drover jumped up in the air and faced the south. I could see that he was shivering. Then the boys off to the west raised a howl, and Drover faced *that* direction.

Scraunch growled and Drover faced us. His head was cocked sideways and one ear stood up. That meant he still didn't see us.

But he was beginning to get the picture. The

ranch was surrounded. I kept waiting for him to run, but he didn't.

Scraunch pushed himself up out of the grass. "You go first. I watch."

"Who me? Well uh, seems to me that . . ."

The hair went up on the back of his neck and there was murder in those yellow eyes. "You go first or I cut throat right here!"

I could tell he wasn't kidding. "I just thought . . . there's no need to . . . I see what you mean, yes, I'll go first."

I stood up. Scraunch threw back his head and let loose the bloodiest howl I ever heard (sent shivers all the way down to the end of my tail, is how frightful it was). He gave me a shove and the attack was on.

Drover heard us coming. He started yipping and jumping up and down, but he stood his ground. I could hear myself talking: "Run, Drover, while there's still time." My voice got louder. "You got no chance, Drover, don't try to be a hero."

Next thing I knew, I was yelling. "Drover, run for the shed! You're outnumbered, they'll kill you, run for your life!"

The little mutt was so scared he was spinning in circles and jumping up and down at the same time. But he still didn't leave his post.

By this time I could see Rip and Snort sneaking up behind him, the moonlight glinting off their teeth and eyes. They didn't look like good old boys any more. They had murder on their minds.

Behind me, Scraunch was screaming, "Kill, kill!"

All at once, something snapped inside my

head. I felt wild and crazy. I headed straight for Drover. I'll never forget the look in his eyes. He was more than scared. He was bewildered, didn't know what was happening to him.

He turned to face my charge. As I flew past him and took aim for Snort, I yelled, "This is it, son, hell against Texas! Fight for your life!"

I caught Snort by surprise and sent him rolling down the hill. That gave me just enough time to catch Rip as he was making a dive for the back of Drover's neck. Hit him in midair and knocked him on his back.

By this time Scraunch had plowed Drover under and was standing on top of him, ready to tear out his throat. I lit right in the middle of his back, got a bite on his right ear, and started chewing.

That took his mind off Drover. He jumped straight up and pitched me off. I got to my feet and he got to his feet, and we faced each other.

"Call off your boys, Scraunch. Let's make it me and you, one on one."

He grinned. "Chicken dog die for this."

I had a little piece of his ear in my mouth, and I spit it out at his feet. Out of the corner of my eye, I saw a light come on in the house. That was my only hope. If High Loper didn't hurry and get his pants on and grab his gun, I was a dead dog.

"Seems you lost a piece of one ear, Scraunch. If you'll come a little closer, I'll work on that other one so's they'll match."

Scraunch cut his eyes toward Rip and Snort. "Get him."

Rip and Snort gave me kind of a mournful look. It was decision time. They had to choose between an old drinkin' buddy and their own flesh and blood.

"*Get him!*"

They licked their lips and swallered and glanced at each other. And they chose flesh and blood. They started creeping toward me.

"Drover," I said in a low voice, "keep 'em off my back, son, or we're finished."

Drover squeaked. He was too scared to talk.

Rip and Snort and the other two coyotes started closing in on me.

"Hunk stupid dog," said Scraunch. "Stupid dog pay with life."

"You could be right, Scraunch, but you've got it to do."

We was totally surrounded and it was every man for himself. I figgered I might as well leave this old life with another piece of Scraunch's ear, so I made a dive at him.

We collided and went up on our hind legs. I boxed him across the nose and he boxed me right back. Made my eyes water. I clawed his lip and he clawed mine. I went for his ear and he went for mine. We chewed and snapped and snarled and growled.

I think old Scraunch was a little surprised that a cowdog could give him such a tussle.

I was holding my own until they jumped me from behind, two or three of 'em, didn't get a good count, but it was plenty enough to finish me off.

They wrestled me down, throwed me on my back, and pinned me to the ground. Scraunch walked up and straddled me, showing his big, sharp teeth.

"Now you die."

He went for my throat and I heard Saint Peter blow his horn.

C H A P T E R

12

THE EXCITING CONCLUSION

S aint Peter's horn had an odd kind of sound. Instead of saying, "toot-toot," as you might expect, it said "bal-LOOM!" And it made fire that lit up the sky, and something went whistling over our heads.

Shucks, that wasn't Saint Peter at all. It was High Loper, and he was standing on the back porch, blasting away with his pump shotgun.

Scraunch had just fitted my throat around his jaws and was fixing to remove it when the artillery opened up. He threw his head up in the air.

"Scraunch hurry!" Said one of the other coyotes. "Kill dog fast!"

Scraunch was going for the throat again for a quick kill when the second load of shot arrived. Loper had found his range, and he distributed a full load of number seven birdshot about evenly through the crowd.

You never heard such yipping and squalling. Them coyotes were jumping around like crickets in a shoebox, knocking each other down trying to get out of there.

All but Scraunch. He backed away real slow. "Another time, Hunk. We meet again."

"Yeah, and so's your old man!" That's the best I could do on the spur of the moment and with a sore throat.

I picked myself up and limped around. I had some nicks and cuts but nothing was busted. I'd come through the fight in pretty good shape, all things considered.

Loper came running up the hill, slipping shells into his shotgun. He hadn't taken the time to put on his jeans, God bless him, which probably saved my life. All he had on was a pair of brown and white striped boxer shorts, his cowboy boots, and a tee shirt with three holes in it, and also some windmill grease. Legs looked awful pale and skinny sticking out of them boxer shorts.

"Danged coyotes!" he yelled. Then he looked at me and—this next part is kind of shocking, so prepare yourself—he looked at me and—still gets me a little choked up, even today—he *SMILED*!

That's right, he smiled at *me,* Hank the Cowdog. I mean, I was just by George overwhelmed by it. In my whole career, I couldn't remember Loper ever smiling at me.

"Hank!" he cried. "You've come back home!" He laid down the gun and came over and throwed his arms around me and gave me a big hug. "By golly it's good to have you . . ." I licked him on the face. He drew back and wrinkled his nose. "Dog, you stink! Where have you been?"

Aged mutton, is where I'd been.

About then, Sally May came up the hill, tying the strings on her housecoat and pushing the hair out of her eyes, which were red and puffy. "What is it, what's wrong?"

"Coyotes, hon, a whole pack of 'em. I bet they were trying to get into the chickenhouse, but old Hank suddenly appeared—good dog, Hank, good dog—and he and Drover . . . where's Drover?"

That was a good question. I'd kind of forgot about him in all the excitement. Then Sally May gave a cry. "Oh no! I think he's . . . he's not moving, just lying there."

I've already mentioned that in the security

business, you can't afford to let your emotions get the best of you. I mean, it's a tough business and you have to be prepared for the worst.

I considered myself pretty muchly hardboiled, but when I saw little Drover stretched out there on the ground, it really ripped me. I mean, the little guy had done his best to protect the ranch, he'd stood his ground under combat conditions. But now . . .

We all went over to him. He didn't move a muscle, not even a hair, and it was pretty clear to me that he was, well, dead. A big tear came out of my eye and rolled down my nose. I had to turn away, couldn't stand to look any more.

Loper bent down and there was a long silence. "His heart's beating. He's still alive."

"Thank goodness," said Sally May.

"Actually, I can't see anything wrong with him. He's got a nick on his nose and one ear's been chewed on, but other than that, he looks all right."

"Let's take him to the house. I'll make him a nice little bed and try to get some warm milk down him."

Loper gathered him up in his arms and they started down the hill. I just happened to be looking at Drover when, all at once, one eye popped open. He glanced around and closed it again.

The little runt was half-stepping, is what he was doing, and he wasn't about to miss out on that soft bed and warm milk. All right, maybe he fainted or something in the heat of battle, sounds like something he'd do, but I could see that he wasn't feeling no pain.

It took him two whole days to get over his craving for warm milk and a soft bed, and he probably could have strung it out another day or two, only he peed on the carpet and got throwed out.

I was down by the corrals when he came padding up. "Hi Hank, what's going on?"

I was working on another case and didn't really want to be disturbed. "Hello, Half-stepper. What's going on is that some of us have to work for a living so that others of us can attend to the milk-drinking."

He shrugged and gave me a silly grin. "I'm feeling much better now, thanks."

"I'll bet."

"What you working on?"

I glanced over both shoulders before I answered. "There's something funny going on around here, Drover. Look at these tracks." I pointed to the tracks but he didn't look.

"Tracks are down here in the dirt, son. That's where you find most tracks, on the ground."

"Hank, tell me something. Did you really join up with the coyotes? I mean, did you really think you could live with them?"

I walked a short distance away and for a minute I didn't answer. "Drover, if I tell you something, will you swear to keep it a secret?" He bobbed his head. "No, I mean you've got to swear an oath."

He raised his right paw. "I swear an oath, Hank. My lips are sealed."

"Okay, I guess I can trust you. You know what undercover work is?"

"Sort of."

"Well, that's what I was doing. See, we weren't getting anywhere with the chicken-house murders, and I figgered the only way we could crack the case was for me to infiltrate the coyote tribe. It was risky. I knew there was a good chance I'd never come back alive, but it had to be done."

"No fooling?"

"That's right. And it had to be top secret. I mean, I couldn't even let you in on it. If them coyotes had ever suspected a thing, it would have been curtains for this old dog."

"Wow. Weren't you scared?"

"Naw. Well, a little bit. Actually, the toughest problem was keeping the women away."

"The women?"

"Right. Drover, you won't believe this, but they was actually fighting over me. I mean, it got embarrassing after a while. Why, one evening these two beautiful women . . . I'll tell you about it some other time. Right now we've got another case to crack. Now look at these tracks. What do you make of them?"

Drover squinted at the tracks. "Well, they were made by an animal, and I'd say the animal walked right past here and left these tracks in the dirt."

"So far, so good. Keep going."

He shook his head. "That's all I see, Hank. I'm stumped."

"Okay, now listen and learn. Them's badger tracks. While we was busy fighting off the whole coyote nation, a badger slipped into the ranch, and I've got an idea that he's still around."

"You mean . . . if we follow the tracks, we'll find him?"

"That's correct."

"Uh oh. Badgers are pretty tough."

"Yes, that's true, but duty's duty. If we start letting badgers in here, before you know it they'll try to take the place over. Come on, Drover, we've got work to do."

He gulped. "Badgers have big claws, Hank."

"You leave the claws to me. I'll go in the first wave, then you jump him from behind. And dang you, if you run off and leave me again, I'll . . . I don't know what I'll do, but you won't like it."

"Okay, Hank. I'll be right behind you."

I put my nose to the ground and started following the trail. It led around the saddle shed and through the garden. Reading the signs, I saw where Mr. Badger had stopped in the garden and dug up a couple of worms or bugs.

I continued east, following the trail through the gate, past the gas tanks, up the hill, and right to the yard fence.

"This is worse than I thought, Drover. He's in the yard. That doesn't leave us much choice. This could get nasty, could be a fight to the death."

"Whose death?"

"In this business, you never know. You just have to give your best for the ranch. Come on, let's move out."

We hopped over the fence. I got down in my stalking position and picked up the trail again.

The scent was getting stronger now. It was *real* strong. Badgers have musk glands, you know, and they leave a heavy scent.

Suddenly I saw him, hiding in a bunch of flowers. I froze. Drover ran into me. "This is it," I whispered. "Good luck."

I crept forward two more steps, went into my attack position, and sprang.

Suspended in the air over the flower bed, I got a good look at the enemy. It suddenly occurred to me that badgers aren't black with two white stripes running down the middle of their backs. They don't have a small head with beady little eyes, or a long bushy tail.

It was a skunk. I had been duped.

I tried to change course in midair but it was too late. Out of the corner of my eye, I saw Drover jump the yard fence and head for the machine shed.

What followed was entirely predictable. I landed right in the middle of the scoundrel. He fired. The air turned yellow and poisonous. My eyes began to water and I gasped for breath.

Sally May's south window happened to be open. Was that my fault? I mean, had I gone through the house that morning opening all

the windows? Of course not, but on this ranch, Rule Number One is that, when in doubt, blame Hank.

I ran for my life and rounded the corner of the house just as Sally May came boiling out the back door. She was armed with a broom and took a swat at me as I flew past. My eyes were stinging so badly that I . . .

You've got to understand that I could hardly see and was having trouble catching my breath. The back porch door was open, and you might say that I ran into the utility room . . . where Sally May had just taken a basket of clean clothes out of the washing machine.

Was it *my* fault that she happened to be washing clothes that day?

"GET OUT OF MY HOUSE, YOU STINKING DOG!"

Well, as I've said before, every dog in this world isn't cut out for security work. It requires a keen mind, a thick skin, and a peculiar devotion to duty. I mean, you put in sixteen-eighteen hours a day. You're on call day and night. Your life is on the line every time you go out on patrol. You're doing jobs that nobody else wants to do because of the danger, etc.

You make the world a little safer, a little better. You take your satisfaction where you can get it, in knowing that you're doing the job right.

The very people you're protecting won't understand. They'll blame you when things go wrong. But that's the price of greatness, isn't it? And if you were born a cowdog, it's all part of a day's work.